His Enemy, His Friend

BY THE SAME AUTHOR

His
Enemy,
His
Friend

John R. Tunis
Member of The Authors League of America, Inc.

William Morrow & Company   New York 1967

For Will Lawless, Tommy Rodd, and
the many other young Americans whose conscience
has led them to prison in these years.

Contents

AUTHOR'S NOTE

This is a book about the conscience of a man.

However, sport plays a part in these pages. The sport dealt with is the game that Europeans call football. When played in the United States, it is association football, or soccer. Since my story is set abroad, I have used the term "football" throughout.

Unlike American football, which is half football and half basketball and neither the one nor the other, the European sport is based upon kicking and passing along the ground. No player save the goalkeeper may touch the ball with his hands. The game is played by eleven men on each side. No substitutions are permitted. There are two halves of forty-five minutes each, and the ball used is round, not oval as in American football. It is a game enormously popular with the young, and draws immense crowds all over the world.

J.R.T.

PART I

Eve of
Battle
June, 1944

Chapter 1

The black-haired sergeant, in the gray-green uniform of the army of Adolf Hitler's Third Reich, sat smoking his pipe on the stone steps of the house. Beside him was a boy of eight or nine in a faded polo shirt, a ragged pair of dark blue shorts, and sneakers so frayed that both his big toes stuck out of them.

The sergeant and the boy were discussing a subject that each considered important and their serious faces reflected this.

"Was that the time, Feldwebel Hans, when you scored the only goal for Hamburg against Stuttgart?" asked the boy.

"Noooo . . ." responded the young soldier. "No,

as I remember now," he went on in excellent French, "that was the year. . . ."

"I know, I know. Don't tell me," the boy cried, excitement in his voice. "I have an account in my scrapbook. Can I show you my scrapbook sometime, Feldwebel Hans? I can? I know; it was the year Hamburg was tied by the Racing Club of Paris, thanks to Bonvallet's last-minute goal. Am I right?"

"Right! Only actually I didn't play in that particular match. A bad knee. And bad luck, too. It was the spring before the war and that knee kept me out of service for thirteen months. Psst . . . come here . . . here. . . ."

He snapped his fingers and held out one hand. A dog was coming toward them, a white and black, short-haired distant relative of a fox terrier. He was a kind of Grande Rue dog, an animal born in the street, heaven knows where and when, a dog of most uncertain heritage. He approached with caution as the big man took the square pipe from his mouth and leaned forward encouragingly.

The dog edged nearer. One glance told you it was a long while since anyone had stroked him, given him a good meal, said a kind word to him. The sergeant reached out and kneaded the back of the animal's neck. Immediately the dog responded by coming in closer. Then he sat on his haunches, seemingly content, for once befriended.

Finally the German rose, knocked his pipe on the

stone steps, and stretched. "Yes, of course you can show me your scrapbook. I'd be interested. Bring it along anytime in the afternoon. Well, we must get the morning report from the blockhouse. It hasn't come yet and the *Herr Hauptmann* will be annoyed."

Together they walked down the Grande Rue, the main and only street of the village of Nogent-Plage, the tawny-haired boy in the ragged shorts and the tall *Feldwebel*. The dog walked between them, his tail wagging.

Since it was a lovely morning in early June, the street was full of people. It seemed as though everyone they met greeted the sergeant. Old ladies in black carrying half-empty shopping bags, housewives with long loaves of grayish bread under their arms, children, especially the boys who invariably appeared when the *Feldwebel* was around, all wished him good day, addressing him as Colonel and speaking in German.

"Guten Tag, Herr Oberst. Guten Tag. . . ."

Although he had told them all a hundred times that he was not an *Oberst*, a colonel, but a *Feldwebel*, a sergeant, and a supply sergeant at that, he responded to their words with an old-fashioned courtesy, speaking in French as a rule, touching one finger to the brim of his stained forage cap in a most unsoldierly gesture, and wishing them good day in return.

"Eh . . . bon jour, Madame Dupont. *Bon jour."*

The old lady in the faded black dress bobbed and ducked her head. *"Guten Tag, Herr Oberst. Guten Tag. . . ."*

There it was once again! How often he had spelled it out for them, sometimes severely.

"Nein, nein, bitte. Ich bin ein Feldwebel, ein Unteroffizier, nicht ein Oberst. . . ."

The people of the village simply smiled and went on addressing him as *Herr Oberst*.

At first he felt this was intentional. After all, with these tricky French one could never tell. Perhaps it was their cynical way of sneering at the fact that the son of a baron, from an old army family, should be merely a sergeant. Occasionally at night when he could not sleep due to the roar of the guns along the coast spattering antiaircraft fire into the heavens, he wondered whether the French were stubborn, stupid, or insolent. As time went on, however, he realized that to the people in Nogent-Plage he represented authority. For them he was a person to whom they could protest, appeal, with whom they could discuss their grievances. It was the *Feldwebel* who listened to their objections to what they felt were unfair regulations of the German High Command along the coast.

Occasionally these regulations were changed. More often they were just ignored by the sergeant and his superiors. It was easier that way. Hence he accepted the greetings of the villagers, and although the military rank they conferred upon him amused his men and not infrequently annoyed his commanding officer, there was little anyone could do with the stubborn French.

The only person who did not call him *Herr Oberst* was the boy in the ragged blue shorts. He felt immediately that the sergeant disliked this and always addressed him as Feldwebel Hans. Perhaps this was how the big German first noticed him. It drew them together; their passion for football cemented the bond.

That day, the fourteen hundredth and fifth day of the occupation of the village of Nogent-Plage by the Germans, a day that was to explode in such violence and change forever the lives of the boy, the *Feldwebel*, and everyone in town, began in calm and quiet. During the long months of the occupation, people in the village had passed and repassed the same troops for days without end. Often even their first names were known to the townsfolk—harsh sounding Teutonic names such as Helmut, Gottfried, and Gerhardt. Over the years, many regiments had visited this hamlet by the sea, the men sunning themselves along the waterfront, or playing football under the direction of the *Feldwebel* on the hard, sandy beach below the cliff. Never was anyone else accorded recognition by the villagers. In fact, they often made fun of the other Germans, not infrequently to their faces. Of all the soldiers, only the Feldwebel Hans was a friend.

He was a friend above all to the boys of the village, because he was a former football player, and especially to young Jean-Paul Varin. Wherever the sergeant went the boy attached himself, following from place to place, often with his pal, René Le Gallec, slightly older and also a *fervent* of football. When the German sergeant played or coached his men, the two boys could not take their eyes off him. The younger, especially, watched with a furious intentness. Unconsciously even his body moved, swung, stopped short, riposted as the big German athlete's did. In vain his mother rang the bell for dinner. You spoke to him and he did not hear. The boy watched, listened to the football talk, played and practiced, went so far as to learn German so that he would fully understand the soldiers talking. Football was his life, his passion, his existence. And the Feldwebel Hans was his god.

Chapter 2

Not only Jean-Paul Varin but all the good people of Nogent-Plage had definite feelings about the Feldwebel Hans. If one had to be occupied by the Germans, the villagers all agreed, it was better that he should be in town.

"Why, the *Herr Oberst* is the son of a baron, if his brother is killed in the Luftwaffe he too will be a baron. Ah, say what you like, *monsieur*, blood does tell. He's part of that old Schleswig-Holstein aristocracy. You know what those people are like."

"How true, *madame*, how true! Besides, he is a man of the world, not merely an ace of the football. He plays the cello and appreciates the good wine of

Bordeaux—and the Normandy cider too, yes indeed. Well, his mother was French, you know, from Sedan. To my way of thinking, he might just as well have been French. *Yes,* I agree. . . ."

"*Eh bien,* his mother was a De Mezière from Sedan. For me he is no militarist, but really a civilized type. He loves the children in town and they love him. Why, *monsieur,* he is their hero. That Varin boy follows him everywhere. You know the *Herr Oberst* was the great defensive back for Bayern of Munich. Once before the war he played for Germany, at the age of nineteen, too!"

"Yes indeed, the boys and girls love him. If I call my René, and he doesn't answer, I know he is watching the *Herr Oberst* coaching football."

"To be sure," interjected a fat woman. "I, for one, shan't forget either when the partisans burned the bridge at Verville and that *Hauptmann* tried to take my husband off to Germany, last year. Ah, no, I told the *Herr Oberst.* Look, my husband was beside me in bed that awful night. He believed me. He even convinced the High Command. He has connections, you know."

Now the villagers were all talking at once.

"Ah, yes, only he could have done it. Why not? A supply sergeant, perhaps, but he understands and respects French culture and French civilization. Naturally, his mother was French. But yet after all, he is German. . . ."

"Yes, *monsieur,* most of these barbarians know neither France nor the French. Well, this man is no stony-faced Prussian such as some we've had stationed in this town since 1940."

"Indeed, *madame,* I recall when the town had to be evacuated, remember, at the time of the big raid on Dieppe. The *Herr Oberst* interceded for us with the *Kommandant* at Caen, you recall? Those who really lived here were permitted to stay. Oh, I am entirely in accord with you. We are truly fortunate to have him here in Nogent-Plage. Truly. . . ."

"Fortunate to have him," that was how the villagers felt about the Feldwebel Hans Joachim Wolfgang von und zu Kleinschrodt, to give him his full name. And he was the one German soldier who seemed to be permanently stationed at Nogent-Plage, which after a while became a rest camp for troops from the Russian front. Usually a regiment or a battalion stayed only a few weeks or a month in this village on the Normandy coast. Then one wet, foggy morning the siren would blow. That piercing noise meant the end of peace and repose for those Germans. From work, from relaxation, from the football game on the beach coached by the *Feldwebel,* they hustled back to their billets, fear in every heart. Early on in the war when Hitler's forces were winning from Crete to Norway and each month a different nation was gobbled up by the Greater Reich, the troops had left for the East singing and cheering.

Then the war was a glorious romp. But two winters in the snow outside Moscow changed this. Now they hardly spoke as they packed and made ready to depart. Sullenly they collected the regimental baggage, silently loaded the transport wagons. When the short, sharp whistle of the *Ober-Feldwebel* rang out, they would line up along the Grande Rue dismally waiting inspection and the command to move off.

"*Achtung!* Right face! Forward . . . hup . . . hup. . . ."

So, off in columns of four down the coastal road to entrain for the East. Nowadays the villagers of Nogent-Plage made an event of this. They lined the streets, watching not without pleasure the grim faces of the soldiers, making sardonic remarks the Germans could not understand.

"*Hein!* They don't seem quite so happy to say good-by, do they?"

"Would you, my friend, with the Russian bear breathing down your neck?"

"Ah, but remember, they used to have nothing but motorized equipment. And all that new English matériel captured at Dunkerque. Remember, *madame?* That has worn out now. Look at those poor old horses. And the wagons falling apart. . . ."

No, the war was no longer glorious for the Germans. Troops of different regiments came and went, only the *Herr Oberst* remained. It was a corps decision to leave him at Nogent-Plage. He was valuable there because he had a quality few of his countrymen possessed. The villagers hated the occupying forces with a fierce Norman hatred, looking and longing for only one thing—the Allied invasion and freedom from German domination. The *Herr Oberst* knew this quite as well as anyone. Yet, thanks largely to him, order prevailed in the village. There were no shootings, no terrorist attacks, no raids as in other towns along the coast. So far as the Germans could tell, the villagers never tried to signal planes or ships. Never had a *Gauleiter* been summoned from Berlin to restore order. In fact, the High Command at Caen had such a good opinion of Nogent-Plage that it considered awarding the town a medal for its correct attitude toward German troops.

Certainly nobody ever called the *Feldwebel* a keen soldier. He obeyed orders and did his duty. That was all. In private life he was a von und zu Kleinschrodt, younger son of an ancient Baltic military family famous in the history of his country. His father had been a Colonel of Uhlans in the First World War. Brought up in the army tradition, he had, perhaps, had too much of it. Not only did the big, seemingly awkward young man look out of place in uniform beside his brisk, competent, Heil Hitlering comrades, but the way he saluted, even his reports, left much to be desired. Many a commanding officer at Nogent-Plage had tried to reform him and given up the attempt. Because of his family and his connections he was no laughing stock—in fact, quite the reverse. Yet he was not entirely in favor with the High Command at Caen.

What attracted the people of Nogent-Plage to the *Feldwebel* was not merely his fame as an athlete, but his agreeable manner, so different from that of many of the Germans. Also there was his love of music. As he was an indifferent soldier, he was an indifferent musician and played the cello, to tell the truth, rather badly. However, he enjoyed playing with Georges Varin, the local schoolmaster and father of young Jean-Paul. Monsieur Varin was an equally bad violinist, but often, when the priest came to accompany them of an evening on the sadly inadequate piano, the three sat immersed in Bach and Beethoven until long after curfew. As a consequence, on those nights, the padre was forced to stay with the schoolmaster until morning.

In the single *café* in town, the Bleu Marin, the German soldiers, playing the harmonica and singing as they drank their beer, were ignored by the French natives. But whenever the tiny bell on the door tinkled ever so slightly and the *Herr Oberst* entered, the fishermen at their *belote* game glanced up and nodded pleasantly. When the curfew sounded they

picked up their cards, avoided the gaze of the harmonica players, and left, bidding the *Feldwebel* good
night on the way out.

"*Guten Nacht, Herr Oberst,*" they said to him.

"*Eh . . . bon soir, bon soir, messieurs,*" he replied.

Chapter 3

Nogent-Plage was like a sheltered spot in a storm. Yet during four long years, though the villagers were never in danger, they heard sounds all day and night that brought the war inside them. One was the endless clack-clack, clack-clack of hobnailed boots on concrete. You heard it in daylight, late at night after curfew, early in the black hours before dawn when the patrols stomped down the Grande Rue. You heard it and soon hated it more than anything else, because it brought the presence of German troops into your home and your heart.

Another familiar sound was the thromb-thromb of the motorized fishing vessels, indistinctly heard, indistinctly seen through the fog which so often covered the coast. Nogent-Plage was a fishing village, and the Germans permitted certain selected fishermen to go out three kilometers—no more—on Mondays and Thursdays. People in town could tell the day of the week by this sound. Naturally, when the vessels returned to the shingled beach below the cliff, a platoon of Germans was waiting to requisition (meaning grab off) their share of the catch. This share was anything up to sixty or seventy-five percent.

If you stood at a certain point on the cliff outside the village, or if you watched from a second-story window of Madame Dupont's house, you could make out the coastal road winding into the distance like a long black ribbon. To use it a Frenchman had to have a special permit, or *Ausweiss*, from the German High Command in Caen.

The road, Route Nationale Number 40, twisted and turned, dipped and rose, as it followed the coast. From Nogent-Plage you could see it stretching for miles, empty of traffic save for a few German army trucks. To travel upon it was, as the French said, "to make the *gymnastique*." Indeed, it resembled an obstacle course, what with the sand from the dunes that had blown over it in places and the holes that had not been filled in since the start of the war four years before.

The whole region was bare and barren, especially in winter, and the winds harsh, cold, strong. They blew so fiercely that few trees survived, and on clear days one had an unobstructed view up and down the coast. The first thing you noticed was the big blockhouse just below the top of the cliff on which the village rested, then other blockhouses at intervals of a mile or so along the shore. They were all sizes, large and small, of gray concrete, which the Germans had forced the French to construct and pay for. These fortifications and others around the *Haupt Kämpflinie*, the great warline, were Hitler's main defense against invasion from the sea.

Here and there along the coastal road were sentry boxes, six feet tall, with conical roofs. Each was large enough for two men and two machine guns. You could see their barrels sticking through the slits on each side. They served to check on traffic and also acted as lookouts over the ocean. Behind the road, away from the water, the dunes stretched for miles, bristling with stakes against parachutists and seeded with mines and booby traps.

To the pilots of the R.A.F. planes Nogent-Plage was a landmark: the first glimpse of enemy-held territory, the first sight of occupied France, the first shriek and whistle of antiaircraft fire, and, if it was night, the first tracer bullets rushing up in the dark. By day the surf crashing on the beach was the first thing they saw below as they roared in out of the mist. Then the rocky cliff above the sand, the village with its single street, and the black ribbon of road stretching away to left and right.

Nogent-Plage itself consisted of only a handful of brick and stone houses, with a gap here and there where a field of fire had been cleared for the guns of the blockhouse. Beyond, in back, was nothing save those endless dunes stretching away to the horizon.

The sand had been there when William the Conqueror set off in his small boats in 1066 to invade England, when Napoleon in 1803 stood on the cliff and looked across to the shores of Sussex, when Hitler on the same cliff in 1940 shook his fist at Britain, the endlessly moving sand was still there. At times the wind blew so fiercely it made one feel that the sand would eventually smother the tiny settlement on its rock jutting into the English Channel.

The German soldiers who garrisoned Nogent-Plage at the start of the war were giant six-footers who had awed the villagers. That had changed. Now the German troops were usually a dismal-looking lot. They were farmer's boys from Thuringia, stunted adolescents or weary old men. But this June morning the people of the town felt uneasy. For some weeks a new breed of German soldiers, a tough battery of Silesians, had been stationed in town. They were a motorized flak unit, highly trained, efficient, equipped with light and heavy machine guns and antiaircraft weapons, continually marching up and down the single street in tight formation. They were shock troops and wanted everyone to know it. They appeared invincible. Their smartness, their discipline, even the way they saluted and their officers returned salutes were impressive.

Above everything, accompanying all comings and goings, was noise—the pound-pound of a hundred pairs of hobnailed boots in unison, the shouts of their noncoms, the raucous calls on the loudspeakers.

"*Machen Sie schnell, schnell, schnell,* hup, hup. . . ."

These men seemed forever on their toes, ready for anything, not war-weary troops resting after months on the icy plains of Russia. They were stationed in Nogent-Plage to kill and be killed. Quite evidently.

Uneasiness hung over the village that day. For one thing there was organized movement in the Bloch villa. This house had been taken by the occupying forces early in the war, because it belonged to a family of Jews long since dead, deported, or forgotten. It made an excellent headquarters in the center of town. Dispatch riders coated with dust dashed up, black leather briefcases under one arm. Engineers worked on the radio aerial on the roof. From the blockhouse came a sudden burst of fire.

Could all this mean, the villagers speculated, that

the invasion was coming? That long-promised, long-awaited, long-hoped-for invasion, so often hinted at in the B.B.C. broadcasts from London called by the natives, "The *Bibbice*." Against all regulations, those Normans, proud, unbending in their attitude toward the occupiers, listened every day to the *Bibbice*. Once Monsieur Varin, the teacher who lived next door to the Bloch villa, had switched his radio on to the B.B.C. wavelength and sat waiting to turn the volume down before the news from London began. Unfortunately he fell asleep. Those first words woke him with a start.

"*Ici Londres. . . .*"

With a bound he leaped across the room and shut the set off. But the Germans billeted in the next house, almost in the next room, must surely have heard it and reported it. He went to bed in a sweat of anguish, lying awake all night waiting for the hammering on the door that meant a German prison camp—or worse.

Nothing happened. The night patrols passed as usual. He heard the low, mechanical beat of their metal heels on the concrete, clack-clack, clack-clack. But no thunderous pounding on his door. The *Herr Oberst*, he guessed, knew what had happened and had arranged things so the German headquarters at Caen did not.

Chapter 4

The Feldwebel Hans, as the boy called him, sat on the stone steps of his billet in the pleasant spring sunshine. He rose and yawned. If the glorious *Reichswehr*, the German army, didn't think much of him as a soldier, he, in turn, didn't think much of the *Reichswehr*. He was hardly passionate about roll calls, drilling, medals, uniforms, saluting, family tradition, army tradition, national tradition—all this seemed to mean little to him. He could easily have obtained a commission through his connections, but the officer corps with its caste feeling nauseated him. Once you get to be an officer, even a lieutenant, he always said, everyone below you suspects you.

Now, with the thin dog near him and the boy as usual at his side, he picked up a clipboard with papers attached, stuck his empty pipe in his pocket, and walked down the Grande Rue and past the sign *Juden Verboten*, with the name of the general commanding officer underneath. The boy did not notice it. That sign banishing Jews had been there four years, which was forever to Jean-Paul Varin. It dated back so far he could not remember when it hadn't been there. His father, he well knew, hated it, but there it was, part of the town like the Grande Rue and the cliff on which the town stood and the ocean below.

Down the street they walked, the French boy and the German supply sergeant. Since they were invariably together, nobody took this as strange. The *Herr Oberst* this morning was hardly Hitler's ideal of a soldier of the Greater Reich. He wore a rather grubby tunic and an ancient garrison cap. If his bearing and general attitude did not express contentment, neither did he appear dissatisfied with his job. The boy beside him, he simply walked along greeting those who greeted him.

Clack-clack-clack-clack, his heels sounded on the concrete pavement. Not clack-clack, clack-clack, short, sharp, brutal, as those of most soldiers sounded, but leisurely, in a slow cadence. At the end of the village the sergeant and the boy reached the vacant lot beside the small church. The thin, lonely dog had

33

scampered ahead and now was in the middle of the road, sitting and waiting. As often at this time of day, the Père Clement, the village priest, was coaching René Le Gallec with a football, or *ballon*, as the French called it. The Feldwebel Hans liked the padre, who had been retired to this backwater when the Occupation submerged everyone. Still active at seventy, he especially enjoyed coaching the football players, for he had been a great athlete himself in his youth.

This morning Père Clement's soutane was tied up around his waist with a coarse rope so he could run. This arrangement disclosed thick cotton under-drawers, heavy black-wool stockings reaching to his knees, and rough peasant boots, badly scuffed and scarred. The padre in his time at Nogent-Plage had developed many young football stars, and the Le Gallec boy with whom he was practicing was the best of all. The *Herr Oberst* stood watching, sucking on his empty pipe, throwing in an occasional suggestion or word of advice. Finally he could no longer resist getting into it himself. Glancing up the street to make sure the new, fire-eating *Hauptmann* commanding the battery was engaged in his office, he yanked off his tunic, snapping a button in the process. The button bounced and rolled. He let it go, intending to pick it up later, placed his tunic on the grass, laid the clipboard beside it, and stepped forward.

Immediately something inside changed. Now he was in his world, in his element, master of himself. His big frame loose and coordinated, he controlled that round ball with his feet almost delicately, pushing a short stab over to the padre, taking it back, turning it across to the boy with an insolent accuracy beautiful to watch.

A spurt past the old man, a short step to the right to dodge the boy, then to the left to catch the pair off balance. All the time he was babying the ball until he had René and the Père Clement so confused that they were ducking first one way, then the other, totally unsure of themselves.

The boy in the blue shorts stood transfixed, his body moving as the *Feldwebel* moved, twisted, stopped, and ran. Two young women going past watched, fascinated.

"Ahhhh, ahhh . . ." they said in admiration. At Nogent-Plage, whenever the Feldwebel Hans played football with the boys a crowd gathered. If he was on the beach coaching the regimental team, a gang of the local lads always sat on the sea wall, commenting.

So this morning half a dozen younger boys suddenly appeared from nowhere the second he began to play. Now he was concentrating upon René's moves.

"No, no, not with the right foot, the left. . . . You must learn to pass equally well with either foot. . . . Don't shoot too soon. . . . Take your time, you have time. . . . Watch that ball . . . and keep your head down. Just watch the ball. Try to remember your teammates are all watching you. They will get it if your pass is a good one. Be careful, don't lift your head. That's better . . . lifting the head is always fatal."

He was no longer the casual *Feldwebel*. Now he had become a wonderful, moving, vibrant force, the great athlete, the virtuoso of ball control, master of himself and his well-coordinated body. When he took the ball to explain what he meant with a cross or a kick, he seemed almost to caress it.

One of the young women watching glanced up the street as she heard a door slam. She saw the new commanding officer step out of the Bloch villa, heard a clicking of heels that resounded down the Grande Rue, observed the sentries presenting arms. "*Herr Oberst,*" she said. "*Herr Oberst! Der Hauptmann kommt.*" The captain is coming.

The athlete stopped instantly, picked up his tunic, hastily put it on, and, reaching to the ground for his pipe and the clipboard, again became the nondescript *Feldwebel*. His garrison cap on one side of his head, he sauntered off toward the blockhouse for the morning report—now an hour overdue.

The dog rose and followed him. At that moment the *Feldwebel* noticed the little Deschamps girl in the middle of the road, about fifteen yards ahead.

36

Evidently the child had strayed from home. There she stood, a target for passing military vehicles. He got down on one knee and called to her.

"*Hier Liebling.*" Come here.

The child turned to look. She was adorable in her faded pink dress, the tiny skirt so short and shrunken from constant washings that it flared out from her thin legs. The big man held out his arms. It was not precisely the typical picture of a German soldier in France in the fifth year of the Occupation.

Instantly the child responded, toddling toward the *Feldwebel*, her arms also outstretched. Then the door of a house banged open, and the girl's mother rushed up to the *Feldwebel*. Knowing she did not understand German, he said in French, "She was in the middle of the street."

The woman took the child from him and began to scold her. Frightened, the little girl started to cry. Together they went into the house, leaving the Feldwebel Hans in the road, the stray dog at his side.

He walked briskly down the street toward the blockhouse, and as he did the dog again rose and followed along.

Chapter 5

By noon a wind had arisen, bringing a chill from the water. The fog was burning off as it so frequently did at this time of the year. Superficially it was like every day in Nogent-Plage, but there were signs of things to come. Formations of large planes passed over the village all morning, roaring off into the interior. What did they portend? Were they the usual attacks on bridges, railroad yards, and airfields around Paris? Who could tell?

Georges Varin, the teacher, sat alone at a small iron table on the pavement before the Bleu Marin, chatting with Monsieur Lavigne the proprietor, a heavy-set man of forty-five with a dirty white apron around his waist. On the table was a cup of bitter coffee made of acorns and heaven-knows-what, the result of wartime shortages.

"Another cup, Monsieur the Professor?" asked the *patron*. Monsieur Varin was no more a professor than the Feldwebel Hans was a colonel, being only the village schoolmaster. However, everyone called him professor since he had studied two years in Paris and was an educated man, one to be treated with respect in the village. He was useful in various ways. For instance, he helped the farmers across the dunes who could neither read nor write by penning letters for them, in a script full of flourishes, to their sons in German prison camps.

Dark, small, stocky, and articulate, he used to wear glasses, for he was nearsighted. Unfortunately they had broken and as no new ones were obtainable, even in Caen or Rouen, he carried a pocket magnifying glass to read the communiques in the daily papers. Whenever he read his forehead wrinkled and his eyebrows rose.

Though accepted by everybody, Monsieur Varin was not popular with the right-thinking, churchgoing part of Nogent-Plage. He was a Marxist and regularly voted the Communist ticket, a fact he never concealed from anyone. Yet even those who disliked him and distrusted his political convictions respected him as a good Frenchman. Had he not fought three years in the First World War, been wounded and returned to combat? Again he had been called to the colors and served through the whole campaign of 1940 as a noncommissioned officer in a frontline unit.

All his life Georges Varin and his family had lived in Nogent-Plage. Early in the occupation he became acquainted with the Feldwebel Hans. They respected each other and had a love of music in common. Slowly over the years they became friends. In times of trouble there had been instances when only the teacher through the Feldwebel Hans had managed to get German headquarters in Caen to listen to the protests of the villagers. Once Marcel Deschamps, the fisherman, had lost his bearings in a dense fog and against regulations did not reach shore until the next morning. Ordinarily he would have been imprisoned for this offense, but the Feldwebel Hans saved him so that he received a warning only.

Few villagers felt there was anything wrong between the schoolmaster and the German sergeant, or considered Monsieur Varin a collaborator and friend of the Nazis. Not only did he despise collaborators, he invariably spoke of Marshal Pétain, head of the French collaborationist regime, as "that old donkey." So Monsieur Varin, though not entirely popular, found his friendship with the *Feldwebel* accepted because it helped the town. In much the same way the *Feldwebel* was accepted by his superiors.

Because of his background and army connections, the *Feldwebel* talked freely and frankly to an old family friend, Major Kessler, Adjutant at Headquarters of the Northern Command. Usually Major Kessler was accessible to the *Feldwebel* on the telephone in a tight moment. The officer in charge of the garrison at Nogent-Plage knew this and obtained favors for himself through his subordinate, the sergeant. On the staff at Headquarters in Caen, they regarded von Kleinschrodt with amusement and indulgence.

"Yes, a strange chap, that von Kleinschrodt. Prefers to remain a *Feldwebel* when he could, of course, have a commission. I remember his father well at Verdun in 1917—a brave man. But this lad is different. Ah well, he saves us a lot of headaches by his knowledge of the people and the region. Nobody knows them better."

Thus each side and all concerned had something to gain by the arrangement, and the Germans officially ignored the sergeant's friendship with the schoolmaster, something irregular between enemies in time of war.

This morning while Monsieur Varin was sitting on the terrace of the Bleu Marin waiting for the arrival of the Feldwebel Hans, the widow Dupont passed by. Her late husband had actually fought in the Franco-Prussian War of 1870, and she was a little dried-up apple of a woman, weighing perhaps eighty pounds, bent and shrunk with age. She always nodded good morning to everyone she met as she proceeded along the Grande Rue. Her black string bag contained four carrots, a turnip, and an onion for her usual midday meal of soup, even now starting to simmer on the back of her stove at home. The moment she saw Monsieur Varin she stood still and beckoned to him.

Reluctantly he rose to meet her. The widow Dupont was celebrated in the village for buttonholing people, usually grasping the men by the lapel of their jackets. Also for her bad breath, a compound of garlic and red wine consumed twice a day for eighty years. Hence the teacher did not regard her approach with anticipation.

As ever, she came close to him, far too close, and seized the lapel of his jacket as if to keep him from edging off.

"Monsieur Varin," she said, "would you perhaps care to do a favor for me?"

"Willingly, *madame*," he replied, trying to disengage himself from her grasp. "Always a pleasure to be of use to you."

"*Ah, bon.* One can always count upon you, Monsieur Varin. I wish I could say the same for others in this town. I mention no names—oh no, no names—but doubtless you are aware to whom I refer. Well, it is about my grandson. You may remember he was sent off to work in Germany when he became seventeen by the Fritz in their forced-labor organization, the Todt organization they called it. He worked in an airplane factory. Such a nice lad, too, respectful and honest, and a good Catholic besides, I assure you. . . ."

"Yes, yes, *madame*." Impossible to bring her to the point, but at least he managed to move back slightly. He was awaiting not only the arrival of the Feldwebel Hans, but who knows perhaps a glass of that good German beer. "Yes, I remember Michel, a fine boy. What happened, Madame Dupont?"

She drew herself up. "*Ah, justement* nothing! You see each month he wrote me faithfully. I'm all he has left. Now for over two months—almost three, Monsieur Varin—nothing. You see he was working in that airplane factory at Altona, near Hamburg, I believe. The British have been bombing it now for several weeks. So I wonder . . . would it be possible . . . do you think you could get me news of him?"

The teacher took out a worn black notebook with a small pencil attached. He wrote: "Dupont, Michel. Aged 17."

"Do you know his number?"

"Six . . . four . . . nine . . . three . . . one . . . zero."

He wrote it down. "Good, count upon me to do whatever is possible. Although I warn you it won't be easy with these fire-eaters that have come to town, these Silesians. But I'll talk to the Feldwebel Hans; he's always helpful. You know his brother is on Goering's staff. I'll try; I'll do my best."

Her aged, wrinkled face beamed. "Thank you, Monsieur Varin, thank you infinitely. I knew I could count upon your help. Ah, what would Nogent-Plage ever do without you? *Au 'voir!*" And she weaved off downstreet, ducking and bobbing to everyone she met.

Chapter 6

The schoolmaster replaced the black notebook in his pocket and resumed his seat at the iron table. Here we are, coming to a crisis in the war, and she wants news of her great grandson, one of God knows how many foreigners forced to work for the Germans. Well, I suppose he is all she has.

At this moment the Feldwebel Hans, clipboard in his hand, strolled up. In warm weather the two often met at noon and the sergeant usually offered the teacher a glass of German beer, which was reserved by the *patron* of the *café* for the German soldiers who had to sign for it. The *Feldwebel*, wiping his face, sat down. The stray dog, still accompanying him, also sat down, panting.

"Hot, very hot," remarked the German. Then to the proprietor, "Two beers, please."

Monsieur Lavigne wiped a corner of the table with his dirty white apron.

"*Merci,*" said the teacher. "*Eh bien,* what's new today? Are we ready for the invasion?" At times he enjoyed needling the young German. "Your compatriots act as though they expected it this afternoon at the latest."

"*Ach,* these frontline furiosos, they are impossible. Always drilling, shouting at each other, saluting. Frankly, my friend, I am skeptical about your invasion. Perhaps, yes . . . it is possible. But look at that blockhouse over there. Nothing can wreck it, nothing. You saw it built yourself. There are ten meters of solid concrete over those guns. Tell me, what shells could penetrate such a depth?" He took a large swallow of the beer.

Enjoying his own beer as a guest of the *Reichswehr* and one not permitted by German army regulations to drink it, Monsieur Varin did not care to contradict his host. But he did not hesitate to voice his doubt.

"*Ah, oui,* you may be right. But after all, my friend, things haven't been going too well for you people lately. One has only to look at the maps. They tell the story of what's happening over there on the Eastern front."

The *Feldwebel* did not wish to betray a lack of

confidence before a Frenchman, so he said, "Ha-ha, ho-ho, let the English come. We are ready for them."

The teacher nodded, but he wondered. Daily he read between the lines of the censored Paris press and followed the maps with attention. As he often told the Père Clement when they were alone, those maps indicated plainly the extent of the impending disaster for the Germans.

It's coming, he told himself. I only want to be here to see it. And surely, he thought, it must come before long or it will be too late. After four years of occupation, of hardships and privation, tempers in the village were rising. That little girl who choked to death last month because no doctor could get through the coastal road. The thin legs of the boys and girls on the street. When you see your children go to bed hungry night after night, well, a man will do anything.

And those strange warships spotted off the coast when the fog lifted suddenly one afternoon. What were they doing? Those massive flights of planes on their daily bombing runs from England. Were they pounding the enemy's lines of communications in preparation for an imminent invasion? Certainly the Germans were on the alert. Signs of crisis abounded. Nogent-Plage was obviously no longer a kind of convalescent area for battered troops. It had been transformed, by orders from Berlin, of course, into

47

a frontline garrison, a pivotal point of the main coastal defense. That was plain. And the battalion of Silesians was here for one purpose. To repel an invasion on the beaches. Somehow the invasion must succeed.

"It must," said the teacher out loud.

Chapter 7

The Hauptmann Seeler, new commanding officer of the garrison, sat at his desk in the Bloch villa. The windows overlooking the sea were boarded up and his only company was a photograph of Hitler. A thin sheet of paper was before him. It was typewritten, marked at the top: *Geheim.* Secret. Below was a heading. *Oberkommando Des Heeres.* From the Army High Command.

This document was about the invasion, which the *Abwehr*, Intelligence Department of the German General Staff, felt to be imminent. It outlined the steps being taken to repel the assault and detailed the disposition of troops and reserves in the neighborhood of Nogent-Plage. The Hauptmann Seeler was on the telephone. His voice was crisp, soldierly.

"*Ja*, Major Kessler, *ja. Jawohl*. . . ."

"In an hour or more, *Hauptmann*, you will receive *Alarmstruppe* II. Do you understand?"

"*Ja, ja*, Major Kessler." Of course he understood. *Alarmstruppe* II was the order for the highest state of readiness against an invasion. The *Major* continued, "We know nothing for certain, *Hauptmann*, but there is a rumor well substantiated that the invasion fleet is at sea. Perhaps, who knows. . . ."

"I understand, *Major*."

"Remember, Nogent-Plage is a pivotal position in the defense of the coast."

"*Jawohl, Herr Major*. We are ready; my troops are veterans. We won't be caught asleep."

"Good. *Heil* Hitler!" The *Major* rang off.

But the *Hauptmann* was perturbed. He rose and stalked the room. A former *Feldwebel*, promoted to commissioned rank on the field of battle in North Africa, he was a fussy, myopic little man with thick glasses, a strict disciplinarian who strutted with authority. He was also a brave officer, as the decorations from his campaigns in the desert showed.

The month before he had been sent in with his Silesians to take over and reorganize the defense of Nogent-Plage, but the situation he had found was worse than he had imagined. Until he arrived, nobody seemed alert and discipline was indifferent. Then there was that *Feldwebel*. The invasion imminent, the Fatherland in the very greatest peril, and what was he doing? Playing football with the boys, greeting civilians in the street. True, the town was quiet for the moment. Yet with all the terrorists about, one could never tell.

The *Hauptmann* trusted nobody and experience told him this was a wise attitude in war. Although his men all said the *Feldwebel* was a great football star, this nonsense must end. The captain, whose fattish body and thick glasses betrayed the fact that he could not run across the street or see a football unless it hit him in the face, was determined to maintain the discipline so essential in this moment of crisis.

Furiously he shuffled the papers on his desk. Paperwork was his soul, his goal, his be-all and end-all. As a sergeant he had been celebrated for his impeccable reports, always forwarded through channels, always on time. Large forms, legible, correctly indented, and sent along to a superior were in his belief the mark of a professional officer. Paperwork, he often told his men, was the other, seldom seen side of discipline.

As for that lazy *Feldwebel*, it made no difference if he was the greatest centre forward Germany ever had. We're at war. I'm in charge here and the troops and the townspeople had better realize it! The more he reflected about the *Feldwebel*, the more annoyed he became. That sloppy soldier's popularity with the troops and, worse still, the townsfolk was a cause of concern for the *Hauptmann*. Why, he thought, everyone knows that but for his family connections he would have been reduced to the ranks long ago.

In any event, it is my duty as his superior officer to report his inefficiency to the *Oberkommando* at Caen. Let them do as they wish. And they will have to do something after they hear from me. I shall make a point of telephoning this morning. But first I must have it out with him, Count *von und zu* Whatshisname. Utter nonsense, that title business. Four years now he has been enjoying himself in the safety of this charming seaside resort while I was up to my neck in sandstorms, fighting with Rommel in North Africa. And promoted from the ranks by the General Bayerlein himself!

He seized the telephone and called the blockhouse beyond the village. "*Unteroffizier Kleinschrodt,*" he said curtly.

The soldier at the other end of the line feeling tenseness in the voice of his commanding officer, informed him that the *Feldwebel* had left some minutes ago with the morning report.

"Which should have been on my desk when I came to this office at seven o'clock today," said the *Hauptmann*. "Punctuality is the first duty of the soldier."

Knowing the officer's passion for paperwork, the

soldier at the blockhouse quickly agreed. The *Hauptmann* slammed down the phone without bothering to reply. He took the papers from his desk, put them into his safe, tried the handle to be sure it was locked, and rose. Straightening his tunic with a sharp tug, adjusting the angle of his cap, locking the door behind him, buttoning the key into the upper pocket of his blouse, he left the office and went out into the street.

The two sentries whirled to attention in unison, presenting arms. The *Hauptmann* flicked a glove carelessly to the visor of his cap in his best imitation of General Rommel. After the dimly lit office the sunlight from the sea dazzled him a moment. His first sight was the *café* almost opposite. What he observed enraged him.

There sat the lazy *Feldwebel*, smugly smoking his pipe and talking to a French civilian. Worse, as the *Hauptmann* noticed on approaching, the Frenchman was drinking beer against all army regulations. Obviously it was German beer. The *Hauptmann* also recognized the man, a teacher in town. He had been pointed out as a possible partisan, perhaps even someone who would transmit intelligence to the British.

The *Hauptmann* stalked across the street, anger flushing his face. The clack-clack of his heels had an ominous sound. Suddenly spotting his commanding officer approaching, the *Feldwebel* rose hastily, too hastily, stepping back squarely onto the dog's front paw. The animal yelped twice and skittered away and the *Feldwebel* lost his balance. He reached out and caught at the table, which overturned, and the two half-empty glasses of beer and the two beer bottles fell to the stone sidewalk. Then, retrieving his balance, he stood stiffly at attention, waiting for the storm to break. It broke with a thunderclap.

"*Was haben Sie*, Kleinschrodt?" asked the *Hauptmann*, ice in his voice. The Iron Cross (First Class) and the Knight's Cross (with a golden oak leaf) trembled on his chest as he spoke. To have to stand here with this lout, he thought. Me, with my decorations and four wound stripes on my sleeve!

But he stood there, saying nothing now, simply looking the *Feldwebel* up and down. As he did so his eye caught one of the bottles of beer on the ground, label up.

"Reserved for the *Wehrmacht*," it said.

The *Hauptmann* looked the *Feldwebel* over angrily. An ancient garrison cap with stained visor was on the back of his head, not over his eyes as regulations stipulated. His tunic was dirty. One button was missing. His shoes were unshined, no doubt from that damned football he played with the village boys. As the *Hauptmann* stood contemplating this sorry figure of a noncommissioned officer in the army of our glorious *Führer*, he reflected suddenly on those

54

deadly battles in North Africa, where for over two years he had risked his life.

The injustice infuriated the *Hauptmann* and his dislike of the *Feldwebel* was so intense that he completely lost control of his temper. For the first time his voice rose.

"What's the matter with you?" he cried, reaching out and grabbing the *Feldwebel's* tunic where the button was missing. He gave it a strong yank and the other three buttons spattered onto the pavement. The tunic fell open and hung grotesquely from the broad shoulders of the younger man.

There he stood, a ridiculous-looking soldier, while the little *Hauptmann*, baring his teeth, spewed out a torrent of guttural abuse. Like all former noncommissioned officers, the *Hauptmann* was an expert in flaying the lower ranks. He did not raise his voice again, or shout, but his words were plain.

"You'll put away childish things, *Feldwebel*. *Kein Fussball. Verstehen Sie?*" No football. Understand?

And he had only begun. For a fact, this *Feldwebel* really did not know what war was, and the *Hauptmann* took pains to tell him so. Monsieur Varin, who had also risen, wanted intensely to leave, but this meant getting round the overturned table and attracting the attention of the *Hauptmann*. So he stood there while the abuse continued. Scornfully the little officer pointed down at the bottles, the glasses, and the spilled beer, now a wet spot on the pavement.

Sweat appeared on the *Feldwebel's* forehead. A drop rolled off his nose. Still the tirade continued, every syllable distinct. Monsieur Varin had served in two wars under officers of every social class, all grades and temperaments. Never had he listened to such humiliation of a fellow soldier. A nasty piece of work indeed, this *Hauptmann*, thought Monsieur Varin, listening. It was quite obvious, as the officer pointed to the overturned table, what was being said. Do this again and you will be reduced to the ranks.

"You call yourself a soldier, Kleinschrodt?" said the *Hauptmann*, utter contempt in his tone. It was a question needing no answer. *"Verstehen Sie? Verstehen Sie?"*

"Ja, mein Hauptmann, jawohl."

The abuse went on for several minutes more, and then without warning the officer half turned and held out his hand across the upset table.

"Papieren!"

It was a command. The teacher fumbled in his coat pocket and yanked out the *Ausweiss* that everyone in the Zone of the Armies was required to carry at all times.

The officer looked at it attentively, then inspected Monsieur Varin up and down. *"Schulmeister, nicht?"*

The Frenchman nodded. Yes, a schoolmaster. He

was tense and frightened, not knowing what was coming, but sure it would be unpleasant. Did it mean he would be arrested?

"*Kommunist, nicht wahr?* In France all schoolmasters are Communists."

A sweeping accusation. But in France many teachers were indeed Leftists and quite a few were Communists. Monsieur Varin stood silently before the German officer, so youthful to him yet so old in battle years. For a few seconds the silence persisted. The teacher could have denied the accusation. What real proof was there? No, even though his life depended upon it, he could not forgo his deep beliefs. So he nodded.

"*Ja, Herr Hauptmann.* I am a Communist."

There he stood, expecting immediate arrest. Now the sweat appeared on the forehead of the Frenchman. Men had been sent to prison for less. But apparently, with this career soldier who obviously knew France, truth was best. The next question would be harder still, because he could never betray his heritage. The officer would ask him if he was a Jew, and one grandfather on his mother's side had been Jewish. As long as France was France and a nation, he was a Frenchman, but to the Germans, if they knew of that grandfather, he would be a Jew.

Surely the *Feldwebel*, with access to the records in the little town hall, knew all about his background, yet had never reported him. Nobody else in Nogent-Plage was aware of his ancestry, for his grandfather had long since died in Lyon.

The teacher stood waiting for the obvious question, but the bespectacled little officer kept silent. He turned, slapped his gloves in a gesture of contempt, and without bothering to return the salute of the *Feldwebel*, stalked down the street. Activity among the soldiers visibly increased as he passed.

Monsieur Varin discovered his legs were weak. He was trembling. Strange, he thought, feeling his heart bump, how the heat grows at noon on a spring day in Nogent-Plage.

Chapter 8

It was afternoon. The farmer Marquet sat on the plank seat of his old-fashioned cart, with wooden slats sloping outward at the top, filled with thick, oozy seaweed—fertilizer for his land. Years of harsh work had made him seem older than he was. But his horse, although thin like every living thing after four years of occupation, had a cared-for look.

The farmer's home was an ancient stone house in a hamlet called La Roye, beyond the dunes in back of town. His wife was long since dead, one son had been killed in the campaign of 1940, another, Pierre, was a prisoner of war in Germany. He lived alone and the people of Nogent-Plage considered him slightly mad, because he had a habit of talking to himself. Twice each year he took the long road around the dunes to the coast for fertilizer.

His only companion was his horse whose name was Sebastian. Why Sebastian? Nobody ever found out. But between them was a bond of affection. The animal seemed to understand his lonely master's needs. And the farmer cared more for the horse, perhaps, than anything save his land, for which he had the fierce possessiveness of the peasant. Between them they would manage to keep the soil nourished and the fields cultivated until the day when his boy would return from Germany.

Slowly the horse pulled the heavy load, up the hill, past the blockhouse, and into the village. Half a dozen young soldiers, stripped to the waist, torsos tanned, towels over their shoulders, picked their way down the cliff to the sea, carefully avoiding the mines and barbed wire. The old man watched with a passionate hatred. How much longer, he wondered, shall we have to look on these well-fed barbarians?

As the cart entered the village, the door of a house at which two sentries were stationed opened and a bespectacled officer stepped out. On his breast was a double row of campaign medals and the Iron Cross. His boots, which reached to his knees, shone in the sun. He walked briskly, shoulders back, every inch of his small frame an officer of the *Wehrmacht*. From the cart, the old man observed that his gaze went from right to left along the street—he missed nothing. On he moved, the Grande Rue now empty save for a few soldiers at the far end.

As the farmer watched he heard a sudden report, like a shot from a hunting rifle, not loud like an army weapon, being fired. At first he was not sure what had happened. To his amazement, one moment the officer was striding down the street, then he was stretched out on the pavement. As he crumpled, one arm fell behind in a peculiar gesture.

A siren went off. Soldiers rushed from a house, rifles at the ready. A tall, black-haired sergeant ran into the street as the siren kept screaming.

All around, soldiers appeared. By this time the farmer Marquet was near enough to see blood on the spotless tunic of the officer who lay, legs outstretched, on the pavement. Two medical corpsmen opened his blouse and listened to his heart.

The tall, black-haired man in charge was exploding orders, pointing first to one side of the street, then the other. A group of soldiers began working the left side. If the door of a house was locked, they pounded it in with rifle butts. From windows on the second floor, shutters opened and frightened faces of women appeared. The same words echoed back and forth.

"*Pas possible!*"
"*Pas possible!*"

Who could have done such a thing? "Impossible! And here in Nogent-Plage!"

Suddenly the farmer Marquet's horse was stopped, and he was yanked roughly to the ground. Two helmeted young soldiers gripped him, two others searched him, but to his surprise did not ask for his *Ausweiss*. They merely hustled him across the road.

He tried to protest. "*Voila*, I only happened to be in town for the moment. I came in from my farm at La Roye for a load of seaweed, for fertilizer. *M'ssieurs* . . . for my land. I live . . . over there . . . back of the dunes. . . ."

Not understanding what he was saying and not caring, they pushed him along. Quite plainly they were taking him someplace. A strange and terrible fear seized him, not for himself but for his horse. The horse was being left behind, his only friend, all he had. The beast realized his master was leaving him and whinnied loudly. Then the farmer heard that familiar clop-clop as the horse attempted to follow.

"Sebastian! Sebastian!" he shouted, twisting halfway around in the grip of the soldiers.

The horse, pulling the heavy cart, fell farther and farther behind, the reins dragging on the pavement.

"Sebastian!" shrieked the farmer, realizing what was happening and where, in all probability, he was being taken. In utter despair he cried out, "Ah, who will take care of Sebastian when I am gone?"

Chapter 9

The *Feldwebel* sank into the chair of the murdered officer. His cap was on the desk before him. He reflected grimly that he had rushed into the street at the sound of the shot without a cap, something the *Hauptmann* had never done in all his army life. Before the *Feldwebel* were the neat piles of orders—orders from field headquarters in Bayeux, orders from Division Headquarters in Caen, orders from the High Command in Berlin. Each pile was carefully clipped and filed chronologically, according to regulations.

He took up the telephone. "Major Kessler at Division Headquarters," he said to the operator in the blockhouse.

Replacing the phone he sank forward with his head in his hands. What idiot could have done this? So great was the misery of the Feldwebel Hans, so keen his understanding of what had happened and, more important, of what lay ahead, that a cry of agony burst from him there in the empty room: "*Ach, du Lieber Gott.*"

The telephone rang. Immediately he straightened up, controlled himself. "This is the Feldwebel von Kleinschrodt."

"Good. Major Kessler here. Have your men been alerted, *Feldwebel?*"

"Indeed yes, *Major*. But I have bad news to report. The Hauptmann Seeler has just been shot by a terrorist."

"Shot? Impossible! I talked to him an hour ago. . . ."

"Yes, *Major*, it just happened. He was dead in the middle of the street when the men reached him."

"Good God! Have you found the assassin?"

"No, *Major*, not yet, but the men have sealed up the village and are making a house-to-house search. They will surely turn him up."

"He must be found, *must* be found, and made an example of. Execute him publicly. Let me talk to the Oberleutnant Schmidt."

"*Herr Major*, he is at the Defense School at Ostend."

"Well then, the *Leutnant*—what's his name?— Wirtig, isn't it?"

"Sir, he is on leave in Bremen."

"All leaves were cancelled as of yesterday. He should be back this afternoon. For the moment you are the senior officer there. To be sure, we will get another officer to you immediately, for with these terrorist raids up and down the coast Schmidt and Wirtig may have trouble returning. Let me see, perhaps the Leutnant Brandt from Blockhouse 242. . . . No, that won't do, we need him for those big guns; he is a specialist. Let me see now. *Ach*, what a time for this to happen! That Polish chap, that Silesian in Blockhouse H98. No, he is a meteorologist and needed where he is. Well, we'll get someone to you as soon as possible. In the meantime, *Feldwebel*, until the criminal is found, six hostages should be taken into custody. Here"—he turned to someone in his office—"get me that folder on Nogent-Plage, Beckenbauer. We were discussing it with the Hauptmann Seeler a short while ago. . . . No, you didn't put it back. Ah, this is indeed a bad moment for a thing of this sort, and with two officers away. . . . Now, here it is. According to this, you have a teacher there named Martin. No, V-Varin, have you not? Right. Do you know the man?"

The *Feldwebel* froze. Faced with what lay ahead, he could not speak. The *Major* continued.

"Are you there, *Feldwebel?* Do you hear me? Those damned terrorists have been cutting wires all along the coast today. I say, are you there? Do you know this man? I can't hear you. Do you know him? It appears he is a Communist. . . ."

Finally the *Feldwebel* found his voice. "Yes, you are right, *Major*. I believe he is a Communist. But never active to my belief. I've known him three or four years now and—"

The other broke in. "They're all alike, all of them, these damned Communists. I've had a lot of experience with them; they don't care a bit for the land where they were born and raised. Moreover, this one is Jewish."

For a few seconds the *Feldwebel* was stunned. How, he wondered, had this ever reached Caen? "No one ever said he was Jewish, *Herr Major*," he suggested tentatively.

"The records show it. I cannot understand how he was ever permitted to remain in that sensitive area all these years. Someone has blundered badly, and I intend to discover who it was. At any rate, get him now. Then there is another chap, man by the name of Lavigne. Runs the *café* on the Grande Rue." He read from a paper. " 'A hangout for dubious characters.' So the report states. Here it is. 'To be watched. Owner was mixed up with terrorists at the time of the Dieppe raid in '42.' We suspect him also. Is there a priest in the village?"

This was too much. In the mind of the *Feldwebel* rose the picture of old Père Clement with his soutane tied up around his waist and those thick cotton underdrawers. "Why yes, *Major*, there is, but actually the local padre is old and inoffensive. Not at all the kind of person to give us any trouble. . . ."

"*Feldwebel*, we are making examples of these men. Was anyone taken at the time of the murder?"

"No, *Major*, that is . . . only an old farmer from the back country. He merely happened to be passing in his cart at the time. He knows nothing whatever. . . ."

"Yes, yes," interrupted the officer impatiently. "You miss the point. Get him. Or did he escape? Did you pick him up?"

"Yes, *Major*, we have him. Only, if you would permit, sir, I'd like to suggest. . . ."

"No comments necessary, *Feldwebel*. Just obey orders. We want six—the teacher, the *café* proprietor, the old farmer, the priest, a fisherman, a boy perhaps. Give them one hour in which to confess. If the culprit is not found and none of them confesses, make an example of them. Have them shot. As a warning, you understand, to other terrorists."

"Yes, *Major*, I quite understand."

"Good. Now for your personal information as you are in charge at Nogent-Plage temporarily. Terrorists have been at work up and down the coast since dawn. This line may be cut any minute. We have patrols out, but the bridge at Varengeville has been blown up and the highway below Dampart completely destroyed. Hence, as far as reinforcements are concerned, you are isolated for the time being. In fact, we are all isolated. Fécamp is isolated. So is Étretat. We are on our own, *Feldwebel*. Is that quite clear?"

"*Jawohl, Herr Major*." It was only too clear. For the first time in his long years at Nogent-Plage the Feldwebel Hans felt the isolation and the loneliness and the danger. They were Germans in a hostile land, about to be attacked from the front and perhaps the rear. The *Major* went on.

"Meanwhile, do not forget. The defense rests in your hands. You are responsible."

"We are ready, sir," he replied resolutely. After all, perhaps a way out could be found. Perhaps, he thought, the invasion will intervene; perhaps they won't be shot.

The *Major* lowered his voice. "For your information, *Feldwebel*, we are advised that the invasion fleet is now in mid-Channel, making about six knots. Most likely they are planning an early-morning assault, hoping to be covered by this fog. It is thick here at present. And at such a moment! *Feldwebel*, only one thing counts. The Fatherland. Our country is in peril. The Greater Reich faces its most critical hour. Your first duty is to round up the six hostages. Unless the assassin of the Hauptmann Seeler is found within the hour, have a firing squad shoot them. Report to me as soon as you have them in custody. Remember, this is not a football game. . . ."

The *Feldwebel* started to say something, but the *Major* cut him short. "I repeat, Feldwebel von Kleinschrodt, this is not a football game. Understand? *Heil* Hitler."

He rang off. The *Feldwebel* rose from the desk. There was tragedy ahead. And he was in the middle of it. To shoot, to kill a friend. In a way, they were all friends. But they were also enemies of his country, and he was in charge at Nogent-Plage. He represented the Third Reich for the moment. What choice did he have? He was responsible for the safety of his men. There were the orders.

"Corporal Eicke," he called out, yanking down his tunic with the same gesture the Hauptmann Seeler had used at the same desk just a little while ago.

First, of course, comes one's country.

Chapter 10

The farmer Marquet half fell, half stumbled down the badly lit stairs. He picked himself up and looked around. He was in the cellar of the Bloch villa.

Opposite was a narrow, oblong, barred window through which came a dampness from the sea. He noticed a fog was collecting, for the wind had died away. On the other side of the stairs another small window gave onto a vacant lot where, he knew, the boys of the village practiced football. There was no glass in either window.

The earth floor of the cellar was moist. The place was filled with odds and ends left behind by the Jewish Bloch family when the war had burst upon them, driving them from Nogent-Plage. Where were they now? What woman had used that rusty sewing machine? What child had played with that faceless doll? Who had sat on that old wooden bench or those chairs without backs?

He slumped down on the bench. The thought of Sebastian with the load of seaweed standing patiently in the street above struck him with such a stabbing pain that he groaned aloud.

"Ah, Sebastian," he cried. "And my poor Pierre in Germany. He will never know what happened to his old father."

The door at the top of the cellar opened and light penetrated the gloom. He glanced up from his misery as Lavigne, in his dirty white apron, was shoved roughly downstairs. The *café* owner, a stout man, picked himself up, rubbing his hip.

"But," he shouted, "I tell you I had nothing whatever to do with it. I was inside washing dishes. I was inside when the shot was fired. I had nothing to do with it." Then realizing that nobody was listening, he saw the futility of his protestations and shook his fist at the door above. "Ah, those *Fridolins*, those barbarians!"

The door opened again, and a German voice said, "*Unter.* . . ."

Monsieur Varin, the teacher, was pushed down. Next came the Père Clement and young René Le

Gallec, with whom he had been practicing football. The priest picked himself up as the door slammed and shouted, "But I had nothing to do with the shooting of the *Hauptmann*. I was playing football beside my church with this boy. The *Herr Oberst* knows I could have had nothing to do with it. He passed by, himself, but a short while before. He played with us. Ask the *Herr Oberst*. . . ."

The door opened once more and Marcel Deschamps, the fisherman, was hurled down. Then a helmeted soldier with a submachine gun stomped downstairs, followed by a corporal. The corporal went over to the teacher, sitting on the bench and rubbing the knee he had scraped during his tumble into the cellar.

"*Sprechen Sie Deutsch?*" he asked.

"*Ja. Ich kann Deutsch sprechen.*"

Then followed a torrent of guttural words, so fast that the teacher had trouble making them out. But he understood enough to put the sense of the remarks into French.

"This village is surrounded," he translated. "Every exit is guarded. Every house in town is being searched. But we have orders from Headquarters that if the murderer of the Hauptmann Seeler is not found —or none of you confesses to the murder—you will all be shot within one hour. These orders are from our *Kommandateur* at Caen."

The German corporal spun around and went up the stairs, followed at a respectful distance by the soldier. The door opened, then slammed shut. A key turned in the lock. Darkness and silence fell over the cellar.

Their eyes gradually became accustomed to the gloom. The farmer Marquet wept tears of despair. Monsieur Lavigne stalked in a rage up and down the dirt floor. The priest, hands extended, asked, "But who could have done such a thing? Surely it must have been somebody from outside the town."

"Yes, certainly, it must have been a stranger. Someone from Évreux, no doubt."

"They will find him soon, and we shall all be released, I am sure," said the Père Clement.

Only Monsieur Varin was thinking clearly enough at the moment to fit the pieces together. It took no genius to guess what had happened—and also what lay ahead. The Silesian shock troops sent in as a garrison, the cutting of bridges along the coast, the soldiers in battle dress—everything told him the invasion was imminent. Some young hothead must have felt this was a chance not to be missed, a chance to throw the garrison into confusion by killing its commanding officer and so to hurt the outfit at this critical instant in the war. To a rifleman firing through the blinds of a second-story window the Hauptmann Seeler was an easy target.

Ah, thought the teacher, those crazy young people, acting as young people so often do, without thinking of others, with no regard for what might happen to those of us left here in the village. Naturally the Germans would avenge the death of the *Hauptmann*. Anyone could have foretold that.

And what difference who the assassin was. If the slayer escapes, we six will be executed. He rose from the bench.

"Come, my friends, the *Feldwebel* is now in command here. He has helped us before, but even if he has authority we mustn't depend on him. He may know we are innocent, he will do all he can at Headquarters, but we must help ourselves. We must organize. . . ."

"Organize!" snorted Monsieur Lavigne. "How can we organize locked in this cellar, with fifty minutes of life left?"

The teacher ignored his outburst. "Look, I have friends up the coast. Things have been happening, things that are the signal I anticipated. And see that fog coming in? What better weather for an invasion fleet to approach the coast? They plan these things, you know; they leave nothing to chance."

Suddenly René Le Gallec, who had been watching from the narrow window, shouted, "They're coming! I hear them! Listen!"

A rumble came from the sea. It grew louder, louder. Soon it turned into a massive roar. Together the men rushed to the window. There in the haze above the low-lying fogbank were planes, planes, more planes than they had ever seen before, so many that they seemed to blacken the sky.

The five men and the boy shouted, yelled, screamed, waved white handkerchiefs through the narrow, barred window, turned and embraced each other. Rescue! Deliverance! Release! Unquestionably those planes were headed straight for the Bloch villa. Already the antiaircraft batteries down the coast were sputtering, then the blockhouse just outside the town joined in. But the planes roared majestically on. Their sound was that of a thousand express trains, a thousand thunderstorms, drowning out the guns.

The invasion at last! Long-awaited, long-hoped-for! They were saved!

Now the planes were directly above, passing overhead, continuing on. None detached themselves to descend on Nogent-Plage. Whatever it meant, wherever they were going, it was no attack upon the garrison of the town. Soon the planes vanished from sight. The noise died away. The antiaircraft fire from the blockhouse stuttered and stopped. One by one, the men left the window. The Père Clement stood staring into space. The farmer sank back again on the bench. Young René Le Gallec crumpled to the floor as if hit by a blow.

The hostages heard the voice of the *Herr Oberst*

up above, giving a harsh, crisp command. It seemed somehow out of character. It had an ominous sound. Then came the stomping of boots. Evidently they were reinforcing the guard outside the front door of the Bloch villa.

Below, in the cellar, five men and a boy faced death in forty-eight minutes.

Chapter 11

When the Hauptmann Seeler had come to Nogent-Plage in the spring that year, he, like everyone else, was immediately attracted to the Feldwebel von Kleinschrodt. Old army family. Nobility. Celebrated German athlete. The *Hauptmann* was impressed. But not for long. He soon had the young man sized up and perceived that he lacked real soldierly qualities. He then tried his best to reform him as other commanding officers in Nogent-Plage had done, to help him live up to the great traditions of his heritage.

Often he used to stand the *Feldwebel* at attention and lecture him. "Kleinschrodt, your trouble is you are like the Americans. I know well the Americans.

For nine years I was head porter at the Schweitzerhof in Dresden and met many of them. Americans want to be liked. They are almost pathetic in this childish desire to be liked. Actually, this is an infantile trait. Americans are children, young and old. It is why they do not make good soldiers. In North Africa we had no trouble with them at Kasserine. We have nothing to fear from them, nothing. They wish to be liked. That is agreeable, yes; it is better to be liked than disliked. Best of all is for a man to be respected. Respect is the basis for discipline—at home, in business, in the Army. Now you are greatly admired by the troops here and liked by the people of the village. But you are not respected. Never forget that soldiers, too, are children. They will never obey you unless they respect you."

These words the *Feldwebel* remembered, for he was finding the *Hauptmann* right about obedience and respect. As he sat at the desk which an hour before had belonged to the murdered man, as he checked the deployment of the troops—his troops for the moment—around the village, as he listened to the telephoned report of a sentry a mile from town, he was amazed at himself. He had assumed responsibility. He had become the senior officer of the garrison at Nogent-Plage.

No time to waste words. His voice was quite as crisp and curt over the phone, his tunic as spotless, as carefully hooked under the chin as that of the late *Hauptmann*. The invasion was at hand. It might come anywhere, any moment, surely by morning. Maybe right now advance elements were trying to land up the coast under cover of the fog. His duty was to his men, to his country, to the Third Reich. He felt attuned to it without thinking.

And the men? There was a change in their bearing toward him, a surprising deference as they knocked on the door or addressed him. A certain respect that was new had crept into everyone's voice. They seemed to be turning to him, leaning on him, trustfully, hopefully. That was as natural as it was for him to assume the duties and the responsibilities of command.

And yet, all this solved nothing. It is not easy to obey orders when the orders are to have your friends shot; it is hard to issue orders when those orders mean a firing squad for your friends. Hanging over him was the thought of what lay ahead. When his mind was busy with other things it was all right. But the moment he stopped to think about it, revulsion took possession of him. Those men were his friends. That boy he had played football with. Obviously the teacher had Marxist leanings. Certainly, we had discussed them together. But brave. Loyal. A good Frenchman. How on earth can I kill a man like him? A veteran of two wars, already decorated upon the field of battle. For I'm the one who has to give the orders to fire. To watch them fall. To certify to their deaths. How can I do this? And that boy! A child really. My God. . . .

He rose and walked up and down the silent, empty room. The Le Gallec boy haunted him, devastated him, destroyed him. How could he? But he must obey orders.

A short, sharp knock at the door and the corporal entered to hand him a radio dispatch from Headquarters. It merely confirmed what the *Major* had told him, alerting all officers commanding troops that a landing, either a feint or the real thing, was expected along the Normandy coast late tonight or early tomorrow morning. He filed it carefully with the other orders.

The telephone rang, and the operator said, "The Major Kessler, *Herr Feldwebel*."

"Von Kleinschrodt? Is that you?" The anxious tone in the *Major's* voice was meaningful. Now the *Feldwebel* began to feel and appreciate the terrible responsibility of command. The *Major* was obviously full of the imminent crisis, obviously worried.

"*Ja*, Major Kessler."

"You were to report to me as soon as you secured those hostages. Have you done so?"

"Yes sir, I was about to call you. They have been apprehended as you ordered." In the back of the *Feldwebel's* mind the same question kept rising. How can I save them? Surely some way must be found.

"And have you discovered the murderer of the Hauptmann Seeler?"

"No, *Major*, not yet, but we are still. . . ."

"Good God, man, how can he escape from a small village? Was the place surrounded? It was? Did you post sentries at all exits? Have you searched the houses thoroughly? Thoroughly, *Feldwebel?*" His tone was packed with exasperation. Plainly he was edgy. "Get him. It's important to teach these partisans a lesson. When they kill, Frenchmen must be killed. No nonsense about it."

"Quite, *Major*. My Silesians here are first-class troops. They have been through many partisan attacks in Poland and Russia. I have three search parties out under the most experienced noncoms. They will dig up the man. Just a question of time, I assure you."

"Good. If not, you understand, those six French must be executed. You understand, do you not, *Feldwebel?*"

"Perfectly, sir. I only wondered . . . I only meant. . . . I do happen to know these six hostages. I can guarantee myself that none of them had a thing to do with the murder of the *Hauptmann.*"

The voice of the older man rose irritably. "*Hier haben Sie nicht mitzureden.*" That's none of your business. "*Feldwebel*, listen to me carefully. These men are an example to the populace. A warning, you might say. If they are all innocent, so much the better. The villagers along the coast must be impressed with the seriousness of the situation and know what measures we shall take if there is trouble. We have shot sixteen terrorists at Abbeville and are rounding up a dozen at Yvetot."

A pause, then the *Major* went on. "You may recall, *Feldwebel*, that in March a band of Italian partisans killed thirty-three of our SS men outside Rome?"

"Yes, *Herr Major*."

"Then you also remember that we were forced to execute three hundred and thirty-five Italians, that is, slightly over ten Italians for every German. At Nogent-Plage we are moderate, only six for one German and an officer at that. We are being lenient, really. Are you there, *Feldwebel?*"

The annoyed voice at the other end persisted. "These lines are being cut constantly now. Did you get that Jewish fellow? What's his name? Are you still on the line? Do you hear me?"

"Yes, *Herr Major*, we got him. His name is Varin."

"And the priest, as I suggested?"

"The *Père* Clement. But truly, *Major*, he had nothing whatever to do with the killing of the Hauptmann Seeler. Actually he is almost eighty. That I would vouch for myself."

The *Major* paid no attention to the *Feldwebel's* comments. "And the *café* owner, probably a Communist also."

"His place is closed up. We have him."

"His name? I had it before, I think. We must have his name. Remember, you are to post a notice after the execution listing these Frenchmen by name and stating that any further sabotage or interference with German forces carrying out their duties will mean that twenty-five more hostages will be selected and dealt with in the same manner. Is that quite clear? Now the man's name. . . . Are you there, *Feldwebel?* Or are you perhaps dreaming of football? This is not a game. You are a soldier of the Greater Reich."

"Yes, *Major,* I am still on the line. The man's name is Charles Lavigne."

"Good! You realize, of course, that the situation is critical. Perhaps *the* most critical moment of the war. The Herr Generalfeldmarschall Rommel, under whom I had the honor of serving two years in North Africa, sent around a secret bulletin last week before he was wounded. He anticipated an attempt at a landing by the English and Americans about this period, with the moon full and the tide high. He urged us all in the strictest terms, *Feldwebel,* not to forget that we must defeat the invaders here, on the beaches. We cannot permit them to get a foothold inland where their superiority in the air will count. We must throw them back at all costs, von Kleinschrodt. You understand?"

"Yes, *Major,* I understand."

"You are in a key position. Your responsibility is therefore great. From that rock—I inspected it myself with the *Herr Generalfeldmarschall*—one can sweep the coast for several miles in each direction. We depend upon you. The Fatherland is in peril tonight; the invasion may burst on us any moment. Germany counts on all her sons, *Feldwebel*, especially those from an old and famous army family such as yours. Remember your father, who died gloriously on the field of battle, and your grandfather, the General von Kleinschrodt. Be worthy of them! Obey orders implicitly. Do not fail. Do you hear me?"

"Yes, *Major*. . . ."

"Good. Now if we cannot get an officer to you, then you must carry out the execution and post the proclamation. As soon as the assassin of the Hauptmann Seeler is found or the hostages shot, notify me at once by telephone. Yes, of course, if you find the partisan who committed the crime, you may release the hostages with a warning. But be sure to take pains to frighten them. I gave you one hour. How much time is left?"

The Feldwebel Hans looked carefully at his watch. "Thirty-nine minutes, *Major*."

"Right! Let me have a report. And *Heil* Hitler!"

The Feldwebel Hans replaced the telephone and sat staring into the empty room. The face of every person in the cellar rose before him: Varin, Lavigne, the Père Clement, Marquet, Deschamps, and the boy. He couldn't even bear to say the boy's name to himself.

At least this much he could do. He pressed the buzzer on the desk. A corporal knocked and entered immediately, alert, attentive, keyed up. And deferential. Amazing how the man's whole bearing and attitude had changed in one hour.

He met the gaze of the soldier steadily.

"Here, Grossman. Take pencils and paper down to those people in the cellar. For messages. . . ." His voice shook ever so slightly, as he said, "They will understand."

Only too well, he thought. They will now realize that their friend the *Herr Oberst* has failed them. They are about to be shot. How could he? they will ask each other. Ah, all Germans are alike, each one will say. Underneath they are all Boches. He is like all the rest; they are all the same, they will say.

The corporal took the pads and pencils, clicked his heels, and went out, shutting the door carefully. The *Feldwebel* put his head down on the desk and wept. He wept for the affection that was gone, the friendships that had failed, the trust that was no more. He cried for those six hostages, but most of all he cried for himself. Because for the first time in his life he saw so plainly and so well that there was no health in him.

Chapter 12

Monsieur Lavigne, the *café* owner, and Monsieur Varin, the teacher, were quietly talking beside the small cellar window that gave onto the vacant lot adjoining the Bloch villa. Despite the commotion caused by the killing of the Hauptmann Seeler, half a dozen boys were playing football there as usual. One was Jean-Paul, the teacher's young son. Occasionally the ball bounced back off the brick wall of the Bloch villa.

The teacher, a shortish man, took a small wooden box and found he could see plainly through the window. A helmeted sentry with a fixed bayonet stalked back and forth before the house. Monsieur Varin looked at his watch. It was an old-fashioned time-piece, a thick, gold affair that once had belonged to his father and his grandfather. He treasured it and wore it attached to his trouser pocket by a worn leather strap. He soon discovered that the sentry walking back and forth in front of the house was out of sight of the cellar window for about twenty-one or twenty-two seconds, eleven going and eleven returning.

"Pssst . . . pssst . . . psst. . . . Jean-Paul . . . Jean-Paul!"

The boy hearing his name, yet not sure where the sound of his father's voice came from, stood perplexed with the ball under one arm. Then he saw that face framed by the little cellar window.

"Papa. . . ."

"Sssh . . . don't look. For the love of God don't look this way," cautioned the teacher. "Wait until the *Fridolin* gets past. Play! Kick that ball!"

The boy instantly obeyed. As soon as the sentry vanished from sight, he kicked the round balloon almost up to the window and leaned down.

"Papa!"

"Sssh, a message. I'm giving you a message for Madame Borel, out on the road to Varengeville. Understand?"

The boy understood. He gulped. "*Ouai, ouai.* I understand," he panted, now frightened at the sight of his father behind the barred window. He took the ball, whirled, kicked it high into the air and raced after it.

The sentry turned, stomped his heels, and went into his act. Except for the little cellar window which the man had failed to notice, all the windows of the Bloch villa giving onto the empty lot had been bricked up. Hence he paid little attention to the band of boys at play. As soon as he disappeared, Jean-Paul grabbed the ball, kicked it toward the window, ran after it, and knelt down to hear his father's instructions.

"Listen carefully. Go get your bicycle. And your fishing pole. Go to the end of town and tell the sentry if he stops you that you are going fishing. Then get to Madame Borel's house as soon as you can, and explain what has happened. That we have been taken by the Fritz."

The lad rushed away as Monsieur Varin stepped down from the wooden box. His face was wet with anxiety. Would the boy get through? Could Madame Borel summon help in time? Is the old truck available?

"Whoof! At least there is a chance. If they get here before the hour is up. How much left?"

"Thirty-six minutes."

"*Eh, juste!* If they get that old Berleit truck they used to derail the train at Montford. The sides are armored. This will take time. Also men and guns to tackle these Silesians. But boldness must pay off. With the old truck they can make it here in fifteen, eighteen minutes. Unless they run into a German patrol."

Everyone listened with attention. Nobody in that cellar had suspected that Monsieur Varin was so close to the Resistance, yet no one was greatly surprised. He seemed to assume leadership.

At this point the door above opened and a helmeted soldier entered, followed by another who stood at the top of the stairs watching with a gun. The first man handed each of the hostages a pencil and a pad of paper. No words were spoken. Nor were any necessary. Each one turned the pad over, examining it. The pads were blocks of old German army orders, blank on the back.

The soldiers left, relocking the cellar door, leaving the six looking down at those ominous squares of paper. Still nobody said a word. Nothing the *Herr Oberst* could have done would have been so utterly final.

"Ah—" A kind of sob came from young René Le Gallec, curled up on the dirt floor. "*Ah, mon père,*" he addressed the priest. "Once you said that someday I would be good enough to play for France. You should know; you played for France long ago. Now I shall never, never . . ." he cried.

"*Chut!*" The priest leaned down and placed his

hand on the shoulder of the boy. "Come, René, we are not lost yet. We are alive. They may send us to Germany, but we shall return. The *Fridolins* are beaten; they know it themselves. See, the *Herr Oberst* is now commanding the garrison. They cannot find an officer to relieve him!"

In a little while everyone except the farmer Marquet was writing. The teacher, crouched against the wall, had his pad on his knees. He wrote clumsily with the aid of his magnifying glass, forehead wrinkled, eyebrows raised in the air.

By ancestry I am at least partly a Jew, although not by religion, for in all honesty I have never attended any synagogue or professed any creed. Yet I feel neither pride nor shame in my origins; indeed I never think about them save in the presence of an anti-Semite, of whom there appear to be many in my beloved France today. First of all, I am a Frenchman. Second, a teacher of French youth. Third, a Marxist, something that, like my origin I have never attempted to conceal. Why should I? My great great grandfather served as a soldier of Napoleon at Austerlitz. My grandfather was wounded in the Franco-Prussian War of 1870. I, myself, was twice wounded in the battles along the Somme in the campaigns of 1917 and 1918. I fought through the disaster of 1940. Because of this or because of my decorations—for the Germans like the French have a military tradition and a respect for soldiers, even their enemies—I have not been sent away from my home here in Nogent-Plage. Hence this France, from which today some of my compatriots would like to exile me, remains the land where my emotions are fixed, my being is centered. I have drunk her culture. I have done my best to defend her honor with my body, to help train her youth. I breathe fully only when in her climate. Next to my wife whom I adore, and my dear son Jean-Paul who is my pride and joy, I count my country as my nearest and dearest.

Adieu La France,
Georges Varin

Across the room, Marcel Deschamps the fisherman was kneeling before the priest. René Le Gallec waited his turn. The farmer Marquet, his head between his hands, sat motionless on the bench. He had written nothing and was muttering to himself.

For how can you write a letter of farewell to a horse named Sebastian?

Chapter 13

René had made his confession, yet his blond head remained bowed. At last he looked up, still on his knees before the padre. There were tears in his eyes.

"My parents don't even know where I am. They think I went swimming. I told them I was going swimming with Michel." Then he voiced the thought of everyone in that cellar. "Why doesn't the *Herr Oberst* do something? Only this morning he told me I should use the left foot more. You remember, don't you, Père? He said I had an excellent left foot. Why doesn't he do something? Now he must be in command here. He has always been good to the people of Nogent-Plage, always. . . ."

He broke down, sobbing, staggered by the brutal injustice of what had happened. Half an hour before he had been free, outside in the sunshine kicking his precious football, the one the *Herr Oberst* had obtained for him. Now he was locked up in the cellar of the Bloch villa, soon to be sentenced to a German prison camp for life. Or something worse, though he could not quite bring himself to believe the Germans would really shoot six innocent people.

Except for the farmer, the men stood talking in knots, Monsieur Lavigne and the teacher leaning against an iron stanchion, the fisherman saying something softly, all shaking a little. All thinking much the same thing. It simply can't be. Things aren't like this. We've never had anything like this before in Nogent-Plage, never. The *Herr Oberst* knows us all. He has worked miracles before. He got us out of trouble so often these past years. Surely he will today.

Their faith in the Feldwebel Hans was touching. Only the teacher was dubious. "You'll get out of this mess," he remarked to the *café* owner. "It will be all right for you, not for me. To the Germans, I am a Jew." He held out his hands in a little Gallic gesture of despair.

At this point they were interrupted by sudden noises overhead. A whistle blew shrilly. The boots of running soldiers above thudded on the floor. They heard the voice of the *Herr Oberst* shouting orders in that guttural German. His voice had changed. Now it was the tone of all the many officers who had garrisoned Nogent-Plage during those long years of occupation.

Far down the street a machine gun gave a stuttering bark, fell silent, barked once more. Monsieur Varin quickly reached the top of the wooden box beside the window. Jean-Paul and the other football players had scattered. Peering out, he could see about fifty feet of the Grande Rue.

The door at the top of the cellar stairs opened with a crash. A soldier stood there pointing a gun at the hostages below. *"Nich bewegen! Nicht bewegen!"* he shouted. Don't move.

Nobody moved. Nobody had any intention of moving. All were far too frightened to move.

The teacher knew immediately what was happening. The Underground was mounting an attack on the Bloch villa in a desperate attempt to free the six prisoners. Unfortunately, the Germans directed by the Feldwebel Hans were ready. Upstairs they began firing out of the windows facing the street. A heavy truck roared past on the Grande Rue, firing in turn.

Below another machine gun went into action. Bullets bit into the walls of the Bloch villa, sending stone splinters flying. Windowpanes shattered, showering glass onto the pavement. Then came bursts of firing the teacher assumed to be from the rescue truck.

Finally he heard it racing off in the direction of Varengeville.

The soldier at the head of the cellar stairs lowered his gun as the noise died away in the distance. The sound of the door closing and the key turning in the lock was painfully definitive. The teacher leaned as far as the little window allowed. He saw German troops moving up the street with the body of a French civilian on a stretcher, the arms of the dead man hanging over the sides. Soon two more bodies went by, then a badly wounded German limping along and assisted by two comrades.

The young football players, not entirely unaccustomed to the sound of machine guns in recent years, returned to the lot and stood watching the activity on the Grande Rue. There was too much commotion in the street for the Germans to pay any attention to them.

"Jean-Paul!"

The boy turned, startled. He grabbed the football from a comrade and kicked it toward the low cellar window, then trotted after it casually. Meanwhile, Monsieur Varin hastily untied the worn leather strap of his watch from his belt and, taking it out of his pocket, tossed it through the barred window on the ground before his son. The boy leaning over for the football scooped up the watch in one deft movement and kicked the ball hard against the house, letting it rebound. His father stood admiring the quickness and ease of the boy's movements, so utterly free and natural, so unconscious, and watched him stuff the watch into his trouser pocket of the ragged blue shorts.

Pray God nobody was looking. Nobody was. The boy raced off home, down the street. At least he was safe. Monsieur Varin stepped down from the box.

"*Ahhhh*," he said, shaking his head.

That futile rescue attempt had cost three lives and completely failed. "*Ahhhh!*" he exclaimed in despair. He leaned down and picked up the block of paper, with his small, precise writing, and slumped to the bench.

The farmer Marquet, his head in his hands, still sat motionless. Still he had written nothing.

Chapter 14

The Chateau de Varennes on the outskirts of Normandy was a busy place that June day. As Headquarters of the Northern Command, it was the nerve center of the defense of the entire region. From a peak of the roof of the Chateau hung dozens of telephone wires that went off in every direction. Camouflaged Mercedes deposited staff officers carrying black briefcases under one arm. Dispatch riders roared up on olive-drab motorcycles. Inside, in a large corner apartment on the second floor that had once been an upstairs sitting room, two staff officers were in earnest consultation.

Behind a desk in this office sat the Baron General von Wenig, chief of staff of the Northern Command.

He was a strong, stocky man with close-cropped hair and a stretched-out mouth used to giving orders and having them instantly obeyed. He looked out through French windows at a cherry tree in blossom and the park beyond, where the grass was green in the spring sunshine.

"Ah, I see. You could do nothing with him."

"Nothing," answered the other man, also a general, tall, tanned, stalking the carpeted room. "Absolutely nothing. He seems to me to exist in a world of his own. However, as you know, it is difficult to talk on the telephone in times such as these. One doesn't dare speak openly with so many listening in. But he seems determined."

"He seems to me determined to die. I've heard medical men talk of a death wish. Now I begin to understand. Doesn't he realize, Klaus, that it is far better to die for one's country under English gunfire than to die from the bullets of a firing squad?"

The tall officer walking up and down nodded. He had a fine, intelligent face, sensitive yet strong. His hair was neatly brushed back from his forehead and this gave him a spare, well-groomed appearance. When he spoke, his eyes had a kind of irony in them, as though he had seen everything.

"Yes, naturally, he knows. He understands the army viewpoint. He must realize this has been done numberless times in the last war. But he cannot bring himself to shoot those six French."

"But Klaus, he knows the necessity for firmness in dealing with *franc-tireurs*. They are enemies of his country. In short, they are murderers."

"True, but he claims they are simply men of the village."

"Makes no difference. They must be made an example of. Otherwise he is a traitor to the Army. Doesn't he see that? If we didn't take measures, we should have riots throughout our rear, with those damned British and Americans firing at us from the sea. This is the overriding consideration. My God, he is disobeying the orders of a superior. There is only one thing to do." The seated man slammed his fist down on the desk.

"Heinrich, permit me. It isn't as easy as all that. This young man believes he is right."

"He believes what? What is right? Does he believe in a duty to the land of his birth? His father died for the Fatherland here in France. Does he believe in tradition? In family obligations? Does he, Klaus? His brother risks his life daily in the *Luftwaffe*, and this young man sits comfortably in a seaside village discussing right and wrong. Let us not waste time on the matter. You and I know that were it not for his connections at home, he would be behind bars right now. Tell me, who is replacing him at Nogent-Plage?"

"A certain Leutnant Rancke from Blockhouse 262B, about five miles east."

The man behind the desk half rose. "Not Rancke. R-A-N-C-K-E?" He broke into an agonized scream. "That fellow was attached to my division at Anzio last year. He is worthless, absolutely worthless! Quite incapable of making a decision on anything, even the smallest matter. My God, what is the *Wehrmacht* coming to? Surely we are down to the dregs if we have to depend on the likes of Rancke! We cannot entrust even a small garrison such as Nogent-Plage to this idiot. Until that *Oberleutnant* gets back tomorrow from Ostend, we must find a replacement. Not Rancke. Meanwhile, as I see it, there is only one thing to do. You are taking over Wissant tomorrow from Straub, right? Then you must leave immediately, stop off and see von Kleinschrodt yourself, persuade him. . . ."

"*Jawohl, Herr General.*"

"At once. You are an older man, a career soldier, not only his family friend, but someone he trusts and respects. He knows you and takes your advice. I shall cancel the order for Rancke and get that man back from Ostend. You take over Nogent-Plage until he arrives."

"But suppose the boy refuses to carry out orders. Suppose he refuses to execute those Frenchmen."

"Then of course you must do it. He should be made to attend as a witness. Everything done strictly according to regulations, *General*. Leave him in command until his lieutenant returns. Then we must

100

court-martial him, as soon that is, as we have repelled the invasion."

The General Froelicher, speeding along in the Mercedes on Route Nationale Number 40 glanced through the haze out to sea. It made him recall the big estate on the Baltic, and the Colonel von Kleinschrodt who had been his dearest friend and a comrade for three years in World War I. He did not like his mission in the least as he thought about the boy. A strange, quiet youth, different from the others, except that he liked football and, I must admit, always played it excellently. I remember once on a wild boar hunt on the family place, he was then about ten or twelve. By mistake somebody shot a stag. The animal dropped, but did not die. I recall he writhed on the ground until one of the beaters went up and killed him. As the blood poured from the stag's head, the boy took one look and fainted. Just like that . . . he fell to the ground. . . .

All the way to Nogent-Plage he thought and worried about the interview to come. Finally they drew up before the Bloch villa in Nogent-Plage. Outside in the Grande Rue, Madame Dupont was hobbling along, nodding and bobbing her head to the other women, the inevitable black string bag in her hand. Observing a vehicle approaching in a cloud of dust, she hastily stepped onto the sidewalk. With these young army drivers one was never safe.

The car stopped with a screaming of brakes. It

was covered with a film of sand that could not obscure its high polish. A soldier jumped out and smartly held the rear door open, clicking his heels together. And an officer stepped onto the pavement.

He was tall, well-tanned, with fine features. There was a row of ribbons on his tunic. She recognized the Ritterkreuz and the Order Pour Le Merité, one of the highest combat decorations of the German Army. Somehow the aristocratic-looking officer and his whirlwind arrival reminded her of the white horses, the plumes, and the gleaming breastplates of the Garde Republicaine of her youth.

Ah, she thought, what smartness, what discipline! No wonder we French could not withstand these people. Surely there is no Army like this. We had only ineffectual troops like Monsieur Varin and young Pierre Marquet, the farmer's son. A nice man, Monsieur Varin, to be sure, certainly, but careless in his dress. And actually, a Communist. He doesn't even conceal it, either.

The smart officer returned the salute of the soldier at the door of the car, saluted again with a glove in his hand as the sentries before the Bloch villa came to attention, and went inside.

In the office of the Hauptmann Seeler, the *Feldwebel* sat by himself where he had been sitting alone for over an hour. The clock on the wall of the silent room showed more than sixty minutes past time for

102

the execution. The *Feldwebel* was more lonely than he had ever been in his life. This loneliness hurt. There was nobody to help, to talk with him, to advise or even disagree with him. The decision was all his. He, too, had heard the big car arriving. Since a car was an event in Nogent-Plage at the moment, it could mean only one thing. Someone from Headquarters had come to place him under arrest, perhaps bringing a replacement to command the garrison. They waste no time in the Army, he thought, as he caught the slamming of the car doors, the sound of the front door opening, the crisp clicking of the sentry's heels. An officer of importance, no doubt the Major Kessler himself. He was ready. The terrible uncertainty was over, the doubts and hesitations finished. The *Feldwebel* felt glad. Standing straight, he put on his cap, yanked down his tunic, and waited for whatever was to come.

A stomping of feet in the corridor. Then the orderly knocked and simultaneously threw open the office door. The *Feldwebel* felt the pride in his subordinate's tone as he announced the visitor. Not every *Feldwebel* was called upon by a staff officer. Let alone a general.

"The General Froelicher," affirmed the soldier, saluting and holding the door open stiffly, then quickly closing it.

The *Feldwebel* had expected anything but this. He

was astonished, bewildered, but he, too, clicked his heels and saluted. The visitor came toward him, arms outstretched.

"My poor boy, my poor boy. . . ." He embraced the younger man. Suddenly a little of the aching and loneliness ceased. Someone cared.

"My boy, my boy. . . ." The visitor stepped back, holding him tightly by the forearm, looking into his eyes.

"Yes, my *General*." He was not far from tears, and the older man realized it and broke in.

"*General! General* indeed! I am still your godfather, am I not? I am still old Uncle Klaus. I had to see you, Hans. This is all so terrible."

He moved away, sat down, crossed his legs, showing an expensive pair of leather boots burnished with age and constant polishing. He took out a cigarette case of gold and extended it. "Have one. They are Turkish. Very good."

The *Feldwebel* refused politely. To have accepted would have been a kind of surrender at the start. However, he pushed a small china ashtray across the desk to his godfather. "You know, you cannot imagine what it means to see you at this moment, Uncle Klaus."

The general, elegant, poised, lit his cigarette with a gold lighter. "Of course. You need help. That is what godfathers are for, my boy. Now tell me. What is this all about? Frankly, I don't understand."

The *Feldwebel* started to talk. He desperately needed and indeed wanted to tell the whole story to this man he loved and respected, who knew him so well, who had been part of his existence since childhood. But it was difficult to begin. Although the Froelichers were old family friends and neighbors back home along the Baltic Sea, they were traditional army people. How could the general be expected to understand? It would make no sense to him.

"You see, Uncle Klaus. . . . I don't quite know how to put it. I have been ordered to do something I cannot bring myself to do."

"Hans, my boy, I didn't come here this afternoon when we are all in such danger to deliver platitudes or preach a sermon. The situation we face is much too serious. I came to save you from yourself."

The younger man nodded. He looked at his godfather, using an old expression of his mother's. "*Um Gottes Willen.*"

"All right. Now tell me everything. I know you have been ordered to execute six hostages. I realize you do not want to do it. But what makes you feel you are more important than the German Reich? Isn't that a bit egotistical?"

The face of the *Feldwebel* flushed. "I don't feel that way at all, Uncle Klaus, and you must know it. I am merely a noncommissioned officer who has never seen battle, the only soldier in Nogent-Plage who doesn't wear a row of combat ribbons on his chest. The *only one*. I am unimportant. I realize this. But, Uncle Klaus, I am me. What I am asked to do betrays myself."

"Hans, my boy, you know you are in the wrong, don't you now? To set your own opinion against that of your country at war? You must see that. You are not in contact with realities, my boy. These people are our enemies. We have occupied them with firmness, but correctly, and with politeness. We have even been lenient with them at times. Yet they still resist. They do not want us here. They hate us, Hans. Many good German soldiers in France and in Italy and Russia, too, have carried out equally distasteful orders. This is accepted military practice."

"I am well aware of that, Uncle Klaus. But once again, I am me. They are other people. I am Hans Joachim Wolfgang von und zu Kleinschrodt. This disobedience of orders is the most difficult thing I ever did in all my life, believe me."

"Of course. Your gesture is a fine one. I respect it. I am a liberal. I can see your side as perhaps some of my colleagues would not. It does you great credit, Hans. But do you appreciate the consequences? You will most certainly be court-martialed for refusing to carry out a direct command. Nogent-Plage is in the front lines now. You cannot have an Army which obeys some orders and doesn't obey others. We obey all orders, the orders of our superiors, the orders of the *Führer*. If you go through with this, nothing I can do will save you. Nobody can save you. And you are one of the young Germans who should lead the Fatherland of tomorrow. Hans, my boy, we look to you to carry out our hopes for the future, to help govern Europe unified by the Greater Reich."

Suddenly his voice became weary. Now the general was no longer a trim, alert staff officer, but an aging, tired man who had carried the burden long years and was appealing to the next generation. The spark had left him. His eyes grew black with fatigue.

Feldwebel Hans moved his head as if in acquiescence. His eyes caught the clock on the wall. It was an hour and a half beyond the time set for the execution, and those six hostages still waited in the cellar.

"Let me say just one thing, my boy. In life, you will find that the things we long for beyond all others, the things we really desire most, are the things we cannot have. Life is that way, full of disappointments for us all. Believe me, nobody escapes this."

Again the young man seemed to acknowledge the words, to accept them, but he did not speak. Finally he looked at his godfather. "My uncle, I hardly know . . . I am not sure. . . . I am not conceited enough to be certain, but in my deep heart I feel it is wrong to kill these six men. It is worse than wrong; it is evil. José Marti said once: 'He who witnesses a crime and does not protest, commits it himself.' "

Now the general was taken aback. "Who on earth is José Marti?"

"He was a Cuban."

"A Cuban!" A lesser breed, the scorn in the tone of the general plainly indicated.

"Yes, a Cuban revolutionary, a great patriot. He is a hero even today throughout South America. I believe he was killed by the Spaniards, I am not sure. Anyhow, he was telling us a truth, Uncle Klaus. By the way, have you ever read Rilke?"

"No." The general felt slightly uncomfortable. He suddenly realized that his godson was in some ways older than himself. Truly this boy had matured. There was a new firmness about the mouth. It was not unimpressive. Here was a twenty-year-old standing up against the authority of the *Wehrmacht*. For a few seconds the general was caught up in admiration of his godson. Why, I was like him as a young man, he thought. I had faith. Whatever happened to me? Why did I never take a stand against Adolf Hitler? Or at least have the guts to resign my commission. Why did I sit back and accept it all as my friends and colleagues did, until we discovered he owned us entirely, and it was too late? Why?

Reluctantly he returned to the somber situation at hand. He pulled a paper from his pocket and took out glasses.

"Hans, my boy, this is a brutal thing we are doing. I agree. But war is brutal. Only by being brutal can we save the lives of the good German soldiers under your command. Sometimes, like yourself, I have doubts. Then I always come back to this, an activity report which I cut out and kept. It is Herr Himmler, then Gauleiter of Poland, speaking: 'If the local population from the Nazi point of view is hostile, racially inferior, or composed of criminal elements who attack German troops in the act of carrying out their duties, all those suspected of supporting these terrorists are to be shot and the women and children deported.' Now we did this in the First World War to protect our troops; we did it here in France at Oradour, we did it at Lidice in Czechoslovakia, and we did it many times in Poland. In Nogent-Plage I consider we have really been most lenient."

"But Uncle Klaus. . . ."

"Wait! Listen to me. It is past midafternoon. We may well have the invasion any minute, at any place along the coast. I speak to you, Hans, in the name of your father whom I so deeply loved. Think! Reflect! Obey your superiors."

"But don't you see, I cannot excuse myself by depositing my conscience with my superiors. Sometimes disobedience is not wrong. Believe me, Uncle Klaus, there are times when it is not wrong. To disobey when your whole being tells you to is obeying your conscience."

"Nonsense, my boy, nonsense! Suppose everyone did that? What kind of an Army would we have? Would we be here? Would we be on the Vistula? Would we hold everything from Narvik to Rome?

What would happen to us if everyone acted as you are doing?"

"What everyone does is their concern. What I do is mine."

"Hans! For the last time, I beg you, no matter what you feel, no matter the rights and wrongs and your inner struggle which I respect, obey the orders of your superior officer. Were you not a von und zu Kleinschrodt, do you know what would happen to you?

"We would tie you to the rear of an army truck and invite you to run until you were so badly cut up you would collapse and give in. That is what we would do. You are betraying your family and your class."

The young man sat motionless behind the desk in misery. Although he loved his godfather and trusted him, although he was so close to him that he felt his presence deeply, he was still terribly alone. But he gave no sign of yielding. A tiny spiral of smoke rose from the ashtray as the cigarette burned out. There was a sad, heavy silence. Neither man spoke.

Then the general rose, his chair scraping the floor. He pressed the buzzer on the desk. The orderly entered immediately, standing at attention before the general.

"Where are the six prisoners?"

"Downstairs, sir. In the cellar."

"Bring them up."

110

Chapter 15

"Are you certain that your watch is at the hour?"

"No. But if it is wrong, the church clock is wrong also."

The only remaining watch belonged to the padre. There were twelve minutes left, then ten minutes, then five. At last the hour was up. The cellar door did not slam open with a crash. No helmeted soldiers came for them. What did it mean? The six looked at each other more easily.

"I feel sure the *Herr Oberst* has persuaded them to do nothing. He knows none of us played any part in the killing. I felt certain, I said so, remember? I said he would get us out. . . ."

Only the teacher was less sure. True, it was not

like the Germans to be late, especially where death was concerned. Perhaps they had caught the murderer. If so, nobody would bother to tell them.

Half an hour passed. An hour. A little more than an hour. Above, telephones rang. Long discussions followed in German. After a while a car screamed to a stop on the Grande Rue outside. How strange, thought Monsieur Varin, that one's hearing becomes so acute at moments like this. He could hear men walking on the hard floor above and distinguish footsteps, the slow pacing of the *Feldwebel*, the quick, brisk steps of the orderlies. Clack-clack, clack-clack, clack - clack . . . clack - clack - clack - clack. . . . Then silence.

They waited, tired now, weary from fatigue and anxiety and tension, drooping a little, all of them. They sat on the hard dirt floor, back against the stone wall, heads nodding.

At last the key turned in the lock and the cellar door flew open. At the top of the stairs stood a soldier with the usual submachine gun in his hands.

"*Hinaus!*" He beckoned them up. Horrible sound, thought the teacher. A horrible sound and a horrible language. I always disliked it and I always will.

The hostages rose clumsily to their feet. They'll probably release us now. They have no evidence against us. The *Herr Oberst* knows we had nothing to do with the killing of the Hauptmann Seeler. Silently, meekly, they went up the stairs one by one.

Just outside the cellar door stood the *Feldwebel* with a tall German officer, elegant in shiny boots, his chest covered with campaign ribbons and combat decorations. The hostages stared at them dully, drained now of all emotion.

The *Feldwebel* signaled a squad of soldiers and turned quickly away, unable to stand the look on those French faces, feeling their faith vanish as he gave the silent orders. The troops formed about them, half leading, half pushing the five men and the boy into the Grande Rue.

When the farmer Marquet, the first in line, was thrust outside, a wild shrieking arose. The prisoners stood for a few seconds blinking in the unaccustomed sunlight. All the women of Nogent-Plage, old and young, surrounded the steps of the Bloch villa in a semicircle. They were being held off by helmeted soldiers with bayonets attached to their rifles.

The women also were armed. They had brought brooms, shovels, pitchforks, and rakes. They brandished them before the soldiers, screaming as the hostages stepped hesitantly into the street.

"Marcel! Marcel! *Mon bien-aimé.* . . ."

"Georges! Georges! *Suis ici . . . ici.* . . ."

The wife of the fisherman tried to break through to her husband. A German soldier seized her and tossed her roughly to the pavement.

At this, like a kind of signal, the women attacked *en masse*. With their shovels and pitchforks, their rakes and brooms, they tried to break through the soldiers and reach the men and the boy. It was impossible for the *Feldwebel* standing on the steps of the Bloch villa to give the order to fire into the melee. To have done so would have meant the massacre of both townspeople and troops. For long seconds the street was in utter confusion.

Run! Run! Run! Run, you idiots, thought the *Feldwebel*, half hoping that the six would burst away in all directions. Surely a few would escape. But they were dazed so they did nothing. The *Feldwebel* blew a short blast on the whistle he had removed from his upper breast pocket, shouted crisp commands, and slowly the women were overpowered and forced back. Pitchforks were seized and tossed aside. The troops formed quickly about the prisoners and the column moved down the street. Only two, the Catholic and the Communist went with heads erect.

My God, thought the *Feldwebel*, I'm marching them to death. Just what I said I'd never do. How did I get here?

From the pleading women who stumbled along beside the column came sobs and screams. Impossible to think coherently, to act intelligently in that emotion. He glanced around.

The General Froelicher was bringing up the rear, there to see the sentence was carried out. He gave no orders, although the soldiers needed no orders. They had done it many times in other, distant lands.

"Charles! Charles!" shrieked the wife of the *café* owner. "Charles! *Regard-moi.*"

"*Ah, mon fils,*" cried the teacher, seeing his wife with the boy at her side. Jean-Paul had the white football under his arm. He was sobbing bitterly, tears on his face. "*Adieu,* Jean-Paul. *Adieu. Et toi, chérie. . . .*"

No man, no woman was shouting to the farmer Marquet. Nor, indeed, did he expect anyone to. But the moment he had come out on the steps of the Bloch villa, his eyes searched the Grande Rue anxiously. What had become of Sebastian? Only a mangy dog trotting along beside the weeping women was now visible. The farmer knew what had happened. The villagers had led Sebastian away. No meat had been available in Nogent-Plage for a long time. They would shoot Sebastian at once.

The soldiers marched in cadence, their boots striking the concrete with that harsh sound. Suddenly Jean-Paul Varin burst away from his mother's arm and rushed up to the *Feldwebel* at the head of the column.

"Jean-Paul!" cried Madame Varin. "Jean-Paul."

Now he was attacking the big German, hitting him with clenched fists, kicking at his legs, weeping and shouting.

Instantly his mother was beside him, dragging him back to the sidewalk. Kneeling down, she held him tightly to her. He buried his head in her shoulder.

115

Quickly the column reached the end of the Grande Rue—and the low wall with its machine guns. A raging tide of women surrounded the troops, held back only by their bayonets.

Each hostage was blindfolded. They knew no hope at last. All illusions were gone. A quiet descended so deep you could hear the half slap, half crunch of the waves on the pebbly beach below. And the sobs of Jean-Paul tearing his body as he clung to the arms of his mother.

René Le Gallec next to the teacher reached out, groping for the hand of the older man. His anguished voice was plainly audible. "Will it hurt, Monsieur the Professor, will it hurt?"

And the reply of the man, distinct above the weeping that now swept the circle of waiting women. "*Non, mon petit*, it won't hurt. You won't feel it." Then the teacher threw back his head and shouted with all his strength.

"*Vive La France.*"

The *Feldwebel* could stand it no longer. Then from behind came the voice of his godfather, composed, clear, crisp. "*Schiessen!*"

"*Vive La. . . .*"

The rifles sounded in unison. They made a queer echo in the fog now approaching from the sea. Startled, the thin dog raced down the road, past the six crumpled figures on the sea wall, toward St.-Valéry in the distance.

116

PART II

Judgment
at Rouen
1948

For most Americans, World War II did not begin until December 7, 1941, at Pearl Harbor. For the French it really began in early May, 1940, with the invasion of France, and the fighting was over in six weeks—almost as soon as it started. Then followed more than four years of occupation by a foreign army, of living under enemy rule.

After the end of the war came trials of various war criminals. Especially remembered are those at Nuremberg, which sentenced to death the most notorious of the Nazi leaders who had not emulated Hitler by taking their own lives: Frank, Frick, Streicher, von Ribbentrop, and others. Here for the first time was established the principle that made not states but individuals answerable to law for acts committed in war.

Less celebrated than the trials at Nuremberg were smaller trials in various lands where the people had suffered at the hands of Gestapo men, Storm Troopers, and even some German army officers. One of them, perhaps the most discussed all over France, was the trial of the Baron Hans Joachim Wolfgang von und zu Kleinschrodt.

It was held in Rouen, the city where Joan of Arc was burned to death by English troops in 1431. In 1499 a building was begun to house the Parliament of Normandy. Later it was turned over to the Law Courts and became the Palais de Justice. Here, several years after the war, the baron was brought to justice for the shooting of six innocent French civilians on the afternoon of June 5, 1944, only hours before Nogent-Plage was stormed under cover of the guns of the British fleet and the *Feldwebel* with almost a hundred of his soldiers was taken prisoner by Canadian troops.

When his case was called he was offered either French or German counsel or, if he so desired, both. He asked for neither. His defense was that he had not shot the hostages or given the order to do so. The order was given by a superior officer, the General Klaus Froelicher, who had been in Nogent-Plage at the time.

Obviously the court found this hard to accept. The General Froelicher had later been killed leading an encircled division at the Battle of St.-Lô. Germans, everyone knew, were not in the habit of disobeying commands, and it was established that Headquarters had commanded the Feldwebel von Kleinschrodt to have the six hostages shot. Moreover, his signature was at the bottom of the proclamation issued to the townspeople after the execution.

The trial attracted attention in all of Europe because the defendant was a prominent athlete, celebrated for his football exploits. The proceedings were short and passionate. Witnesses, mostly inhabitants of Nogent-Plage, including several widows of the men who had been killed, testified against him. Their quiet bitterness was impressive. It was shown that a Hauptmann Seeler commanding the garrison at Nogent-Plage had been shot to death in the street on June 5, 1944, the day before the invasion of Normandy. The baron, then an ordinary *Feldwebel*, or noncommissioned officer, assumed command and was ordered to seize six hostages and confine them. This he did. Unless the murderer was discovered, he was to shoot the six within the hour.

Was there a superior officer present at the execution? One had come to town, yes. Madame Dupont and others had seen him arrive at the Bloch villa in a big Mercedes. But was he actually present when the six hostages were shot? Nobody was sure. After all, there had been all that swirling, screaming confusion when the women had attacked the German troops with pitchforks and rakes. And later, during the execution itself, all eyes had been on the condemned six. So if he was there, nobody could recall seeing him. And anyway it was the *Feldwebel*, at the head of the column, who had marched the men down with the firing squad, and presumably he had given the order for their death.

Because of the fame of the accused, public interest in the trial was great. Foreign as well as French journalists were present. One American correspondent, perhaps more imaginative than his colleagues, sent on to New York a vivid description of the baron as the Butcher of Nogent-Plage. The title stuck. So that was how all the witnesses and spectators in the high-vaulted fifteenth-century courtroom of the Palais de Justice at Rouen came to think of him.

A *hussier*, or bailiff, in knee breeches, stood up with a document in his hands. He read rapidly.

"WhereasontheafternoonofJunefifthnineteen hundredandfortyfourtheaforesaiddefendantcaused todieatthehandsofafiringsquadthefollowinginnocent FrenchciviliansRenéLeGallecGeorgesVarinCharles LavigneLouisMarquetMarcelDeschampsandthePère ClementthereforeyouHansJoachimWolfgangvon undzuKleinschrodthavebeenconvictedofthemurder oftheabovenamedsixFrenchmen.Thedefendantwill comeforwardtobesentenced."

The spectators half rose to watch the black-haired man stand and, with shoulders squared, step into the box. He was in civilian clothes, wearing a sports jacket with leather patches on the elbows that told of happier times. It fitted his muscular frame tightly because of its age, but still it became him. The witnesses, especially those women in black wearing black veils, watched with icy anger. Nothing could bring back their men.

The bearded judge with the little red-and-white cap upon his brow leaned forward.

"Has the defendant anything to say?"

The courtroom was quiet. Since the baron had hardly spoken in his defense except to deny his guilt, it hardly seemed likely that he would talk now. But after a moment he nodded.

Arms folded, he said, "*Hauptrichter*, I have only this to say. I am not guilty of the charges. I did not pronounce the order to have the six hostages shot. In fact, I disobeyed that order. Had Germany won the war, I should have been court-martialed by my own countrymen and faced a firing squad myself."

A murmur ran through the courtroom. The bearded judge gavelled sharply for silence. The defendant resumed.

"No, I did not kill the hostages. I did not kill them because the order to do so offended my conscience. And when conscience and the state conflict, the conscience of a man must take precedence.

"But if I did not obey this order, I perhaps obeyed others I should not have obeyed. As my chiefs were wrong to obey the orders of a madman. We were all guilty, *nous étions tous des assassins*. Hence we must pay the price. I am ready. But first, I wish to say this. Someday you French and"—here he looked at the row of correspondents—"you Americans, even you Americans who were victorious and therefore think such a thing is impossible, someday you may also murder, torture, drop bombs, and kill innocent people in the name of some cause or in the belief that you are somehow defending your country while fighting in a foreign land, as we did."

Once again the gavel sounded. The judge said, "The defendant will now be sentenced. Hans Joachim Wolfgang von und zu Kleinschrodt, acting for the Court of Cassation, I sentence you to ten years at hard labor. Sentence to begin immediately.

"The case is now ended. The court is dismissed."

PART III

Soldier
from the Wars
Returning
June, 1964

Chapter 1

Germany came to a full stop that day. France also ground to a standstill. So did Scandinavia, the Low Countries, and lands far more distant from the ancient city of Rouen, where the contest was to be held.

Saturday afternoon is a busy time in Europe. Not that day. Factories everywhere shut long before the kickoff. Stores, shops, offices closed. Theaters emptied. Traffic subsided. Each metropolis suspended its normal activities.

The only crowded places were bars, *cafés, bistros, bierstubes, trattorie*. People poured into them to watch the game on television. Twelve countries had requested the match live for their national networks. All Europe was aroused.

127

Why this excitement over a game of football? First, because it was more than a game. This contest pitted the Stade Rouennais, champions of France, against Bayern-Munich, champions of Germany. Hence it was a French-German contest, the first time since the end of the war that a team from across the Rhine was to play in a country which had suffered more than four years of occupation, deportation, and even starvation.

Everyone who knew football realized there would be a twelfth man on the field for France: the French crowd in the stands.

But chiefly the match was important because of two outstanding players. Who in all France could forget that the greatest of German goalkeepers was the man who had shot French hostages during the war and been tried in the very city of Rouen? And if the Munich team was led and inspired by its veteran captain and goalkeeper, the French also had their star. He was a young, nervous, magnificent forward named Jean-Paul Varin. Everywhere in France he was called the *"comingman français."*

In cities, towns, and villages throughout the land, thousands of boys addressed a football the way Jean-Paul did. Young men of every age tried to run like him, shoot like him, pass like him. He was far better known than any politician or movie star. When you saw men with their heads together in a *café* or a

128

train, they were not necessarily talking about business or politics. More likely they were discussing Jean-Paul Varin.

Now he would come up against the great German veteran. After the Feldwebel von Kleinschrodt had gotten out of prison, serving six years of his ten-year term, he had felt lost. His brother had been killed in action in the last week of the war. Many friends were also gone. Some were still in Russian prisoner-of-war camps. His mother was dead. His family vanished. The great estate on the Baltic was in ruins, devastated by the Russians, then occupied by the British. Finally one night the main house and other buildings caught fire and burned to the ground.

Where could he go? What could he do? He did the thing that came naturally, the thing he liked best of all—he turned to football. It was a poorish living, coaching junior teams in and around Hamburg. For several years he practiced continually, running to get his legs back. At first it was difficult for him to keep up with his boys when refereeing one of their matches. Gradually his legs returned. So did his form. Often he played goal. As goalie he could see the entire field, watch all the boys in action, coach them as they ran and passed. With a whistle around his neck he would blow twice to stop play and race out to correct their mistakes.

The boys learned. They liked the challenge of the

man in the goal before them. They improved. Before long his teams began to win. They were noticed, and he became known as the animator of football among the youth of Germany.

After several years in which he kept attracting attention, the manager of Werder of Berlin had the idea of asking him to try out for the team. He did, playing superbly. As a goalkeeper his age—he was then thirty-eight—mattered less. True, he had slowed down, but in goal he was magnificent. He knew all the techniques of the attacker. His reflexes were still keen, his coordination perfect, and he could outlast anybody on the field. When he stepped in for Werder-Berlin the team won nineteen straight games.

Next he transferred to Bayern-Munich and helped them win a title with his superb play in goal. He soon became mentor and team leader. Within a few years he had twelve caps—that is, he had played twelve times for his native land in international competition. Once he traveled to London, where his defensive play won a game against West Ham, the English champions. By this time he was God the father of German sport.

Now, with his team, he was returning for the first time to France. The small stadium at Rouen was, of course, sold out. It normally held fewer than 20,000 people, and although 10,000 extra wooden seats had been added, hordes had to be turned away. A makeshift press box had been constructed for the dozens of sportswriters and radio and television reporters. They came from as far away as Oslo in the north and Rome in the south. Suddenly this sleepy city on the Seine had become the sporting capital of the entire continent. Dozens of commentators speaking every language in Europe appeared, all concentrating on that afternoon of football.

So wherever you happened to be that day you heard their rapid-fire commentary—across the street, from the *café* on the corner, from every open window and every open door.

In France and Germany middle-aged men stared at television screens, dreaming dreams of their youth. Young men and boys saw themselves on other fields for other teams: Rotweiss of Essen, Real of Madrid, Benficia of Lisbon. No other single event in the history of sport had ever before united so many millions in so many disparate lands.

Yet who could forget one salient fact? Certainly nobody present at the game, no one watching in France, was unaware that the father of young Jean-Paul Varin had been murdered by the Feldwebel von Kleinschrodt in a small Normandy village twenty years ago. Everyone knew that as a boy of seven or eight he had witnessed the killing of his father. There it was. There it remained in the hearts and minds of French men and women. Try as they would, and

131

many honestly did try, they could not expunge the bitter memories of that June day. The story of the shooting had been brought out in the trial. It had burned into them all. You might try to thrust it aside, you might say it was ancient history, an incident of two decades ago, best forgotten. You might make an effort to ignore it.

The fact, however, was that the greatest goalkeeper in the history of German football was the hated symbol of French defeat. He was the Butcher of Nogent-Plage.

Chapter 2

The German team arrived several days prior to the game and put up at a small hotel on the Seine nearly six miles from Rouen. Each morning before practice they went for a five-mile walk across country.

"Stamina, that's what football is all about," the baron said to them. "The team that is the freshest in the last five minutes usually wins. We took the league because we outlasted better teams. Look at me, I'm over forty, but I believe I could outlast some of you young chaps because I've still got my legs. You fellows with your Porsches and Karmann Ghias will lose the use of your legs someday."

They realized he was right. Had they not seen him

run in a practice match when occasionally he came forward on the field to coach the offense?

The afternoon before the day of the game he took each man out alone for a stroll in the countryside, discussing the tactics to be used, the makeup of the French team, how they should handle their adversaries, and especially what to do about Varin.

"We should allow Varin and the French to do the running. Let them play their game and hold them. Nothing is more discouraging than to play your best and not score. Then every few minutes you boys turn it on. When the opportunity arises, go. You can score goals, Sepp. Turn it on, suddenly, unexpectedly. These boys are dangerous here in Rouen before their own crowd, but they can be beaten."

Never did he mention his notoriety as the Butcher of Nogent-Plage, which would make the match so bitterly fought. He did not need to. His teammates were as aware of it as he was.

Early that evening, before dinner, a press conference was arranged in the dining room of the hotel. Television cameras pointed directly at the baron. On a table before him a dozen microphones had been placed to pick up his words. The journalists and commentators kept after him from every corner of the room, talking in four or five languages, some needling, others more understanding and less insistent. He replied evenly to each man, pausing a few seconds to think before responding, never permitting himself to be ruffled by the most hostile remarks. Even when a blond Dane asked whether he was pleased to be back in France again.

Those queries he did not care to answer he turned aside tactfully, discussing only matters pertinent to the game. His adroitness at handling this rather unfriendly group of newsmen made you appreciate his qualities. You could understand why he had been chosen to assume responsibility and lead his team into action. How, he was asked, would Germany defend against the marvelous French offense, which nobody to date had stopped?

He thought a moment and then replied slowly, "France is a nation of individualists. You would expect the French players to be a great team, of course they are. To win in their league they had to be. I saw them play last year at Dusseldorf—they are magnificent attackers, finely trained, skillful, never letting up. But, nevertheless, though they are a team of champions, they are also and primarily a team of individualists. By that I mean they sometimes ask a man to do it on his own. Now our tactics are somewhat different."

As he spoke, the room grew unnaturally quiet. Here was a football captain talking frankly, freely, and yet modestly about his opponents and the tactics he would use against them the following afternoon.

His cool confidence was contagious. Reporters bent forward to catch every word. All present knew of whom he was thinking: Jean-Paul Varin, the greatest centre forward ever produced in France.

Then a small dark Italian spoke. His German was excellent, his tone unpleasant. "Do you fear Varin?"

A collective sigh, a sort of "aaahhh" rose. One reporter stopped midway in the act of lighting a cigarette. Another, who had stood up to rush away and file copy to meet an early deadline, quietly sat down again.

Surely this was too much. This was pushing him too far. This was unfair. The tall figure behind the table did not stir. But watching closely, you could see his right hand tighten around the stem of a microphone.

The newsmen waited for his answer. Would he explode in anger? Would he suggest that he had been tried, convicted, and imprisoned by the French for a crime he had not committed. Or would he ignore the question entirely?

For endless seconds he stood motionless. Then his mouth opened and in flawless Italian he replied. "We Germans greatly respect the French team and all their players. We do not fear anyone."

Chapter 3

The football played abroad is a sport in which there is less violence than the football played in the United States. Names are taken by the referee, players are cautioned, but only occasionally is a man sent off the field for deliberate roughness. Since there is no substitution in European football, the loss of a player is a severe penalty because then a team must play with only ten men against eleven. To lose a goalkeeper or an important forward can be disastrous.

But if there is usually no great amount of violence on the field in games between top-class teams, violence persists in the stands. In Spain and Italy especially, the fans go crazy, and football riots are front-page news everywhere.

Recently a French sporting newspaper published an advertisement which read: "Monsieur Collet, the referee of the football match last Sunday between the Racing Club de Calais and the Stade Roubaisienne, wishes to thank the members of the Calais team for saving his life after the match." A joke? No, it happened. Football abroad is a serious affair. Many teams keep a car under the stadium during their games. The engine is running and a chauffeur sits at the wheel to rush the referee to safety if the home team loses.

Sometimes riots get out of hand. Fixtures in the stands are uprooted, rocks, bricks, and even seats have been torn loose and hurled onto the field. Players have been shot at during a contest. In the coalfields of Yorkshire in the North of England, they throw what is called a Barnsley snowball. This is a lump of coal covered with snow and hurled at an offending referee.

The day of the game at Rouen, a great broad river of people flowed through the turnstiles of the stadium. Young people, old people, poor people, rich people, people of all kinds and classes. Men in expensive Alpine hats, men in cloth caps and work clothes. Thousands of women and girls were there, for the game had breached the sex barrier because of the attraction of the young football genius on the French side. Speculators were getting fifty dollars a ticket outside, and selling all they could obtain.

138

Many Germans carried huge banners of greeting from across the Rhine. *München Grüsst Frankreich. Berlin Grüsst Frankreich. Bremen Grüsst Frankreich.*

Then outside the stadium came an explosion. A car had caught fire. Two men leaped from it and were lost in the crowd. Successive blasts rocked the car as one bunch of firecrackers after another went off. The fire was put out by the Rouen Fire Department—luckily on hand and waiting—and policemen, who then searched the parked vehicles. Many were filled with fireworks and other explosives, guns, even small cannon to celebrate the victory or perhaps menace the winners. These cars were seized and put under guard.

Inside, the chanting, cheering, and sometimes jeering crowd roared at everything. Hawkers passed through the stands selling programs, beer, and souvenirs, from T-shirts to ties and blazers with France or Germany embroidered on the pockets. At last the German team trotted single file onto the field. Thousands of horns blew triumphantly, thousands of Germans waved red-black-and-gold banners with drill-hall precision, left-right, left-right, left-right, all in unison.

"Hoi, hoi, hoi," they shouted. This was their team, the one that had shut out Torpedo Moscow for the first time. The noise from the stands beat down on the field like heavy surf pounding on sand or shale.

The Germans wore blue shorts and white jerseys. Then the French appeared in dark red jerseys and white shorts. Immediately thousands of tricolored flags sprang up on the opposite side, fluttering in a kind of irreverent pattern of color in the afternoon sunshine. All over the stands strangers addressed each other.

"There! That's Jules Garnier, Number four."

"That's Bonnet. . . ."

"That's Laffont, six. With the bandage around his left knee. He was hurt against Lille, you know. They said he might not play."

"Which is Varin?"

"Varin! You've never seen Varin! He's Number two. That's him, the tall boy who looks like an angel."

"Ah, so that's Varin. We only saw him once on television. We're from Marseille."

"We've come all the way from Bordeaux. Ah, there's Rudy now."

The referee, in blue shorts, high blue stockings and a blue jersey, appeared below. He was Rudolph Stampfli, a former fullback for Zurich and once a Swiss international who spoke four languages. He was known as the best referee in all Europe, firm, decisive, noted for his quick decisions, and possessing a vast knowledge of the game.

The two captains conferred with him, the tall

baron twitching the brim of his gray cap, that lucky cap he had saved since before the war and wore only in an international match. Garnier, the captain of France and the massive outside right who had competed fifteen times for his country, shook the hands of the Munich goalkeeper.

On the sidelines the two teams waited. The tension built up and up. The players longed for the game to start. After the opening rush downfield they would forget everything—the crowds, the shouts, the whistles—everything save that round balloon at their feet.

It'll be all right, each man told himself. I'll be fine as soon as play begins.

Chapter 4

But it did not start. The band played "The Watch on the Rhine," the German national anthem. Then the "Marseillaise." Still the game did not start. Time passed. Seconds were minutes, minutes seemed as long as a day. The athletes did what athletes the world over do in such circumstances. They leaped high in the air, squatted and squatted again. They kicked their feet out and up. They bent over, twisting at the waist, to touch the ground on either side. Some walked around nervously, unable to stand still.

Nothing happened. From above, the French stands whistled and shouted. The delay was torture for everyone. The captains standing beside the stocky

142

referee straightened up. But the ball stayed under the arm of Rudy Stampfli. The crowd all over now yelled for action.

"*Commencez!*"

"*Anfangen!*"

"Why don't they begin?"

"*Commencez! Commencez! COMMENCEZ!*"

It appeared that the jam at the entrance gates had been so great, the confusion in the stands so widespread, that many spectators had not yet found their seats and were blocking the aisles. Hence the kickoff was delayed. The wait seemed forever.

The referee looked at his watch. Six, seven minutes had passed. Eight. Nine. Ten.

His arm went up. He snapped his out-pointed hand toward the small circle at midfield. The whole stadium roared as the teams rushed out, eager for action. One Frenchman crossed himself as he stood poised for action, not for victory, no, but to acquit himself well that day.

Suddenly the whistle sounded. The start proved that this was no match for weak hearts. France kicked off and pushed the ball gently to Bonnet, a wing, who kicked it far ahead to the right, a pass beautifully spotted. Varin set off at full speed as though the ball were already there. Sepp Obermeyer, Uncle Sepp, the German veteran who had been assigned to mark Varin, was caught flat-footed by that amazing and effortless burst of speed. You had to play against the boy to appreciate him.

Here it was, the very first minute of the game and the famous French attack built around their young star centre forward, around ball control, around pace and more pace was taking over.

"VarIN . . . Var . . . IN . . . Var . . . IN . . . Var . . . IN. . . ."

The cheers rose, burst into an unearthly roar as the tall Number 2, taking the ball back on the pass, snaked his way through the German defense, stopped short, twisted, curled the ball around his feet, raced ahead, evading the defensive backs. A dart, a dash, a stop, a pivot, a turn, a twist, and he was nearing the goal.

"*Regardez!* Look at that! *Allez, Jean-Paul, Allez! ALLEZ! FRANCEFRANCEFRANCE. . . .*"

In millions of homes all over the nation millions of men and women were screaming the same refrain. "*Allez! Allez,* Jean-Paul. . . ."

The crowd on the French side of the stadium went wild. They were in a frenzy as that red-shirted Number 2 bore down on the goal.

The huge knot of photographers behind the left goalpost steadied themselves, feet wide apart, straining forward, cameras at their eyes. Before the goal the tall German veteran waited coolly. He tugged at his cap, watching the French boy pass the ball to a teammate and receive it back. The baron was wise and knowledgeable. Better than anyone he knew the importance of his slightest move. He had to guess and guess correctly. Waiting just long enough, he raced out, bent low, and scooped the ball away as the Frenchman slammed into him and went flying over his shoulder to land with a crash on the turf. The shock of their collision could be heard all over the field.

The German was older, more solid, more inured to blows of this sort. Besides, anticipating the shock he had braced for the boy's onrush. Yet even he staggered from the impact before he could rise, straighten out, and kick the ball far down the field. The French player who had tumbled as though shot from the sky lay unconscious upon the turf. The whistle blew loudly.

For a moment there was silence in the stadium, a silence more violent than the roaring that had preceded it. Then a screaming chant rose from the French side. What had been in the back of their minds all afternoon now came out in a torrent of sound. It wasn't that the French—both present in the stadium and elsewhere watching—lived in the past. But that the past lived in them.

"Le Boucher! Le Boucher! Le Boucher!"

Chapter 5

The French stood and chanted. Now a shrill, derogatory whistling could be heard, too, mixed with boos. A brick arched up from the crowd and landed on the field. Another entangled itself in the nets of the goal, then another and another. Immediately armed policemen with riot guns appeared. They fanned out, facing the stands and scanning them from the edge of the field. They were tough cops in boots and helmets, ready to toss out anyone who disturbed play.

No more bricks were hurled, but the chanting and whistling continued. "Le Boucher! Le Boucher!"

Nothing more fell onto the field, but the shouting and whistling continued.

Players frequently know nothing and hear nothing the moment play begins. Often the baron had to be told which opponents had scored a goal on him. But this time it was hard for him not to recognize the name they were calling him. Every Frenchman and Frenchwoman in the stadium or watching on TV was sure that the baron had injured Varin on purpose.

"*Ah, quel sale type, quel salot!*"

But then, everyone agreed, what would you expect? Those Germans just have to win at any cost, at any cost.

The long legs of the boy stretched out on the ground stirred ever so slightly, the first sign of returning consciousness. The baron walked over to see how he was, but the French players who had formed a circle around Jean-Paul, refused to step aside for him. Now the boy sat up, his head in his hands. Yves Robin, the French trainer, and Garnier bent over him, slopping water on his face. They helped him up and he walked a few steps, plainly dizzy. There was a cut on the right side of his forehead. Blood ran down his cheek.

The crowd noticed it immediately. "Aaaahhh . . ." they cried. But what would you expect from the Butcher of Nogent-Plage?

The trainer gave the boy something from a bottle to drink and wound a bandage around his head. Jean-Paul raised his hands in protest, but the trainer, paying no attention, taped the bandage securely.

The baron leaned against a goalpost. He had in his time survived many on-field collisions, but this one had shaken him up, too. His body ached. He bent over, panting, then straightened up. The French stands jeered. However, he went to Varin and patted his shoulder. Jean-Paul nodded. He was all right.

His fans shrieked for a penalty kick. Even the captain of the French team stood protesting. But the referee shook his head. Varin jogged up and down to cheers from the stands. Finally he indicated that he was ready.

The referee placed the ball near midfield, and the game got under way again. For a while the play was negative, nervous, and uncertain. Because of the injury to their star the French momentarily lost their poise. The Germans at once seized their chance. Quick, direct, with passes short and sure, their game well coordinated and neat, they broke dangerously into French territory. Schroeder, their centre forward, shook loose, and after a series of passes had a great opportunity to the left of the goal, and young Helmut Herberger, the punch of the German team, crossed over, reached the ball, and drove it with all the force of his instep toward the goalie. Bosquier, the Frenchman, made a magnificent save at point-blank range. The ball, however, spun from his grasp.

Big Schwartz, following up, kicked it again. Again Bosquier saved, diving at the ball just in time. The French stands were ecstatic.

Two great teams, two superb goalies.

As play progressed, Varin slowly regained his top form, and as he did the French side came to life, now attacking without mercy, using long, articulated passes. So perfect was their position play that a teammate was invariably reaching the ball on those passes at the exact moment. Their surge downfield was a joy to watch.

Even the Germans were impressed. So were the sportscasters. High on top of the stands a wooden platform had been constructed over supporting uprights—a precarious perch for cameramen and commentators. The little Italian television man from Milan who had been so rough with the baron at the press conference was speaking what seemed a thousand words a minute into his microphone. As Varin, taking and passing the balloon, bore down on the German goal, he screamed, "*Ah, il furia francese. . . .*"

The French attack, especially that of Varin and the wingbacks, was built on speed and more speed and tinged with that Frenchiness of the French, containing all their national characteristics—dash, drive, cerebration. Whereas the Germans felt that ball control was vital at all times, the French took risks and brought them off. When the Germans obtained the balloon, they kept it until it could safely be passed to a teammate. Their passes were short, accurate. Yet, watching, one felt that there was power in their game, that they were a team that could explode at any time.

Of the two, France was seductive, artful; Germany stronger and more brutal. Never again did Obermeyer allow Varin to get loose. He kept continually at the heels of the French star, for he also was fast. And although France always seemed to be attacking, forever banging away at the German goal, the Germans' defense was so tight that after that first sortie it looked as if the home team was never going to score. The crowd watched, cheered, groaned as two national temperaments, two styles of play, unfolded below them. Millions all over Europe sat transfixed by their TV sets.

His youthful, dynamic energy fully regained, Varin dominated the field, perhaps even more noticeably because of the white bandage around his head, a kind of helmet of Navarre. If you don't learn football by the time you are ten years old, you never will. Jean-Paul Varin, the French centre forward, had learned it truly and well as a boy from the Père Clement, once an international competitor for France. He had learned it also by listening to and playing with the *Herr Oberst* or, as he called him, the Feldwebel Hans, now calmly awaiting his onslaught in the German goal.

Chapter 6

Nobody can play truly inspired football in an empty arena. It was the roaring mass of the crowd that brought out the greatness of the teams and their stars. There were twenty-two players on the field, but the concentration of the stands was on two: the baron and Jean-Paul.

The struggle became a duel not between France and Germany, but between the veteran and the youngster. Often when the German had blocked a sudden thrust or caught a stinging kick, he would tease Varin by holding out the ball, then dodging a few steps, bouncing it a few times in the penalty box as he ran forward. Then would come a sly roll-out to a forward at one side or that great zooming kick, high, far back into French territory.

Thousands of local fans who had no tickets, but had come to the stadium hoping to pick up one at the last minute, stood patiently outside in the sunshine, willing merely to listen to the noise from within.

They could tell with exactitude whenever Jean-Paul was off and running by that surge of sound from the French stands, that rising roar: "*Allez*, Jean-Paul! *Allez! Allez! Allez!*"

It would reach a frenzied pitch, a crescendo, as the boy neared the German goal, then subside into a vast, collective groan as the baron made another acrobatic catch, another desperate save, and the German stands cheered.

The two defenses were equally effective, but the French side had a diversity that their opponents lacked. They kept the home crowd up by the fluidity of their play. On the attack they pressed forward constantly, always assaulting the enemy goal. On the defense they contracted smoothly. The amazing accuracy of their passing was such that each man seemed to have eyes in the back of his head. They could send and receive a ground pass at full speed. Suddenly, without warning, would come that quick cross to a teammate, perhaps with his back to the German goal, who instantly whirled and shot.

But if the French were the more thrustful, tearing

holes in the German defense at thirty yards out, still they could not score. That big panther in the goal, leaping from side to side, blocked everything.

He deftly deflected a stray shot over the crossbar, coolly punched another ball around the corner post, then dived to prevent a score on a low kick from Bonnet, the French winger. The Germans were technically superb. They were the epitome of controlled power. Yet over all was the baron, completely in command, vigilant, watching each man, calling crisply to his teammates as the play fluctuated up and down. He was the soul of the German side, the great tactician, the Rommel of football.

A truly magnificent player, even the French spectators agreed. But for him France would have scored and scored again as the forwards pressed the attack. In the sense that they were in German territory most of the time, the French were winning. They held the upper hand. But what good is it to dominate a game if you cannot score?

With a top-notch goalkeeper, even second-rate teams find it easy to defend—if, that is, they do nothing else. But the tactics of the Germans were by no means solely defensive. Strong, intelligent, they waited until the precise moment to strike—then struck hard. Their team had no offensive genius like Varin. But they had perfect ball control with short, accurate passes, unspectacular but impossible to intercept. It was football that demanded much of a man: patience, skill, and fitness. Especially fitness.

On the home team was that great centre forward of France, that boy with the white bandage around his head. Centre forward is one of the most important positions on a team. Rarely is it given to a youngster. But Jean-Paul Varin had an old football head on his young shoulders. He could move either way, pass with either foot. His control was so perfect that he was always able to do the unexpected: kick to the goal the instant an opportunity presented itself or pass to an unmarked teammate. Moreover, he had a peculiar trick of moving the ball up to an adversary, showing it to him, and then slipping away, almost magically, with the balloon still at his feet. There was an electric quality about his moves that communicated to his teammates and the crowd alike.

He was indeed *"guele d'ange,"* angel face, as the French called him.

There was a studied elegance, a kind of joy in his bearing on the field. Despite the injury he had suffered, he kept smiling. On the white bandage was a spreading reddish stain. He had a French fineness of feature that was seductive. Tall, frank, outrageously spoiled by nature, he was the boy that everyone wanted for a brother, that every woman would have liked for a husband or a son.

His character, too, made itself felt. You were attracted to him despite yourself. If you had never seen him play, you came to the field determined not to enthuse over Varin. In five minutes you were on your feet, shouting like everyone else: "*Allez*, Jean-Paul! *Allez! Allez!*"

Even the Germans applauded his skills, his moves on the field so marvelously thought out in advance.

"*Ein fussballwunderkind*," they said to each other.

"*Ja, ja, ein fussballwunderkind . . . ja, ja. . . .*"

The interchanging forward line of France, whirling, twisting, shifting, moving in a pattern to the exact spot on the field, kept passing the ball from one teammate to another. Sepp Obermeyer, who had been so completely fooled in the opening sequences of the game, now stuck to Varin unerringly.

As one German in the stands remarked to a friend, "Sepp stays with that Frenchman so closely he'll end up in their dressing room at half time."

Varin's function was to set up the goal, to create the opening for others as well as score himself. Sometimes he was the decoy forward, quite as important as the man with the ball. Then next time, with everyone expecting a pass, he would turn suddenly and strike himself. Often the Germans knew exactly what he was going to do—only they didn't know when.

On the field the referee blew his whistle for a German tripping and gave France a free kick from thirty yards out. His manner was firm and decisive. You could see he was a no-nonsense kind of referee.

The ball was beyond the penalty box. A wall of huge Germans stood before Garnier, the French captain, as he went back to kick. He tried hard to curve the ball around them and did so, but Borkowski, the big blond Silesian, knocked it away and the baron had no trouble reaching and holding it. That penalty could have been costly, he thought, as he rolled the balloon out to Otto Schoen, his winger at the left.

Play continued, chiefly about the German defensive zone. Suddenly the referee's whistle sounded again. It was half time. The game came to a halt. Neither side had scored. The players, shoulders hunched with fatigue and strain, bodies consumed by the fierce intensity of the struggle, slumped off to their dressing rooms.

The first forty-five minutes of the match had seemed to last forever. In another way, it seemed that only a few minutes ago they had all filed out onto the field, waiting for play to begin.

Chapter 7

Not much was said in the German dressing room between the halves. What was there to say? The players
were too weary to talk. They sat on the benches,
heads bowed, panting, speechless. Only the baron
moved from one to the other, praising a stop made, a
pass executed, a kick here, a thrust there, warning
someone about a single careless moment of play. The
men listened to their captain. Otto Schoen was the
man who spoke up. The veteran winger raised his
head. He saw the lines in the goalkeeper's face, recognized the tremendous responsibility that was on him.
Rising, he put his arms around the baron.

"Hans, if you keep playing like this, we can beat
that team."

Time to resume play. They clattered across the wooden floor of the dressing room, down the long concrete corridor, and onto the field. Their appearance brought the German stands up. An ecstatic display of red-gold-and-black flags greeted them.

The second half began. The French pressure, sharp, incisive, continued. The baron's goalkeeping was still amazing. He was a cross between an acrobat and an octopus. Unerringly he sized up each play coming toward him, guessed where the ball was going to go even before it was kicked. His arms, his big hands, his long fingers seemed to attract every shot to his grasp. Now a hard one was knocked over the crossbar, now a cannonball drive at his ankles was cleanly stopped and held. Often the kick was going away from him, but he reached and saved them all.

In that saturated bombardment of the German goal it looked so easy. But that was his trademark, making those stops look easy.

Why, you said to yourself, watching from the stands, I could have held that one. I could have stopped that kick, held that ball. You forgot, unless you knew the game, his experience and that knack of anticipating each play. Above all you ignored his amazing reflexes, which contributed so much to his skill and to keeping Germany even with France as the second half moved along without a score.

Equally steady on the high ones just under the

crossbar, the short, quick stabs from in close, or those long, hard kicks beyond the penalty box, he contained them all. The ball would come at him out of a melee of arms, legs, and feet, so hard it stung his hands. But he held it. Gradually the sportswriters, the television commentators in the makeshift press box, their field glasses to their eyes, began to realize the German goalie was extracting the poison from the French attack.

Still the waves of attackers in red jerseys bore down on the baron. Each time he held them off, cleared the goal, saved Germany. Each time the dagger of France was blunted. Once Robert Laffont, the French inside left, made a superb thrust. From a mix-up in the penalty box he cleared a kick low, hard to the corner. The French stands went wild for it seemed a sure score. Somehow the baron got across, stopped the balloon with outstretched hands, an impossible stab. It got away from him and dribbled along the ground. Two French players were on the ball but he reached it first, quick as only the great player can be. Diving for it, he rolled over and over on the turf, the ball cradled in his stomach. Both sides cheered his great preventive football.

To make such a save is the mark of genius. A little while before the French were calling him a butcher. Now they applauded along with the exultant Germans. The French are like the rest of us. They wanted terribly to win that match. But, like the rest of us, they were not insensitive to talent when they saw it. What they were watching was football genius, and every French spectator knew it.

After a corner kick for France from which nothing resulted, Germany now moved to the attack alertly. France fell back, regrouped, ready, anxiously watching. For a moment the baron stood panting, weary, one arm outstretched against a goalpost. However, the swing of fortune was shortlived, the respite soon over. Following some infighting around the French goal, Varin stole the ball and was off, moving with those long, effortless strides across midfield and into enemy territory.

There it was, that quick, accurate flick to Bonnet, the burst of speed into open country ahead for the return. The young centre forward took a cross back, and the moment he stopped the ball made a sudden, unexpected flip to Carpentier, the inside right, just behind him. Again that roar rose: "France . . . France . . . France. . . ." Once more they threatened.

Carpentier charged in. Before the goal, Borkowski of Germany, one of the stoppers of the Munich defense, a great oak of a man, made a slashing slide tackle which jarred the ball loose. But in the full momentum of his drive the Frenchman was a truck with the brakes gone. What happened was partly, perhaps, resentment over the blow to Varin, but mostly explosive exasperation at the so-near-and-yet-so-far game that France had played all afternoon. Carpentier leaped into the air and collided with the baron.

When the French go in they go in hard. Away flew the gray cap the baron wore. He fell to the ground as the referee raced over, blowing his whistle and pointing to Carpentier.

First a hush. Then a half moan swept the German stands as they stared at their man stretched out on the ground. Without that goalie Germany would be helpless. Everyone knew it.

Each spectator seemed to have felt the shock of that collision. Along the German side of the stadium they watched anxiously. The unvoiced thought hung in the air: if he is finished, we're finished. We're through if the baron has to leave the game. Every eye focused upon the knot of men around the figure at the goal line. The baron writhed on the turf as the trainer bent over him. He twisted and turned. His knees came up slowly. You could see the agony on his face.

The men watched him solicitously. After a while they helped him up. He leaned over, straightened his body, staggered a little, shaken from his second blow of the afternoon. Cheers came from all over the stadium. He walked around unaided. The whole crowd burst into applause.

Once or twice he half stumbled as he took his place, jogging back and forth along the goal line. Then he washed his neck and face with cold water, toweled himself, picked up his cap, and went back into the goal. The German banners waved triumphantly.

This time the ball went to the far end with Germany getting a free kick. Otto Schoen stood ready. A free kick from close up is dangerous for the defense. Will it be a soft, lofted ball or a hard, swift kick? He kicked. The ball just cleared the crossbar above the goal. No score. A tremendous roar of joy exploded from French throats, an enormous groan from the German spectators.

Aching all over, holding on to one goalpost, the baron watched a play developing at the far end. He saw no crowd, heard nothing, felt nothing but the danger ahead. Every instant his eyes under the old gray cap were fixed on that white balloon moving toward him in a kind of inexorable pattern.

France was coming on the attack with Varin upon the ball. For a second he lost it in a welter of legs and feet at midfield. Then once again that graceful, moving athlete came up with the ball.

"Look out, Sepp! Watch that winger, Horst! Watch him! Watch him, man, WATCH HIM. . . ."

Now it's over to Varin . . . to Bonnet . . . stop him, Fritz, stop him . . . back to Varin . . . a cross to Garnier almost intercepted . . . no! Back to Varin, who is breaking through. . . .

The kick was low, hard, into the far corner of the goal. The baron jumped for it with all his great strength, his body parallel to the ground, touched the ball, missed it, and lay prone on the turf.

Pandemonium! Horns. Cheers. Red-white-and-blue flags aflame in the sunshine. Cheers. Shouts. Yells. France! France! France!

Jean-Paul turned and raced away, both arms high in the air. Skip-skip, leap-leap. He somersaulted on the grass in joy; as he came back he was surrounded by several teammates who hugged and kissed him. Others rushed up to embrace him. It was all his. After the shots missed, the kicks blocked, after those endless and hopeless assaults it was his own, his first goal in his first international match for France.

Can happiness be greater?

All the while the big German goalie lay flat on his stomach, pounding the turf in anguish with his bruised fists and knuckles. Helmut Herberger, the winger, young in years yet somehow old with insight and understanding, recognized the agony inside his captain. He raced over, knelt beside him, bent over and caressed the man's shoulders.

Finally the baron rose. The whistle of the referee sounded. Germany kicked off, a little push to the right. The game was practically over now, for only three minutes remained. The stadium was a cockpit of noise, nerves, passion. The thousands in the stands lived and died a hundred deaths. The delirious French

163

shouted and screamed with joy. They even joined in as the baron coolly repulsed another thrust.

"Ah, let's admit it. He is a *brave type*, strong, stubborn. *Un maître*, a master. *Un vrai* champion."

But up in the press box the old hands all said, "Watch out, France. The game isn't finished. Be careful. Any team that scores first and camps on a one-goal lead may find itself in trouble if it merely tries to defend."

Chapter 8

France! France! France! France! A great, lusty, full-throated roar. The French felt victory ahead. It was over, done, almost through. Triumph was there for the taking.

Jules Garnier, the captain and winger, and every man on the French team knew, however, that the Germans were still dangerous. Perhaps they knew it even better than those experts shaking their heads from side to side in the press box. Because they had lived through many games won and lost in the final minutes. They had often felt the inconsequence of fate dealing them an unexpected blow or turning disaster into sudden victory.

Keep moving! Keep up the pressure, they urged each other. Whatever happens, don't let down now.

The soccer player needs the stamina of the long-distance runner, the reflexes of a boxer, and the concentration of a golfer. But it wasn't so easy after ninety minutes of attacking football. France had been setting the pace; now legs ached, feet were leaden. To run required an effort of will, to race down the field was torture. Every French forward had lost a little drive, a tiny part of his reflexes. But they did not give in or let up. Those red jerseys still pressed forward around the German goal.

As ever, the baron controlled the ball with that fluid beauty which was his alone. He seemed to wait until the last possible second before flinging his big frame at the white sphere. But he needed every inch of his height and every ounce of his power to reach those kicks, those punches from the feet and heads of the French forwards. Now it was a shot diverted to one side, now a ball that ricocheted off his chest. The French gave him no respite. They realized to a man that another goal would put the game on ice. Yet they could not hammer through.

The contest was a football match no longer. It was war. It was nation against nation. It was those two eternal rivals, France and Germany. It was life and death in the afternoon. Play grew rougher as the seconds passed. Rough tactics begot rough tactics. Only

166

one thing counted—victory before the final whistle blew.

"France! France! France!" chanted the French spectators in unison. Only a minute and a half to go now. The Germans, backs against the wall, still fought stubbornly and savagely. They could not match the consummate artistry of Jean-Paul Varin. They simply had no forward in his class. But they were still a team and team play counts. They remained solid players, unshaken by misfortune, refusing to accept defeat until the whistle blew.

A slow ball, a bobbler from thirty feet out, came bouncing irregularly toward the baron. He knew how often a mistimed shot can catch a goalie off balance. Carefully and deliberately he went down on one knee, watched the French forwards rushing toward him, then rose, stepped calmly aside, and booted the ball high in the air and far downfield.

There was a mix-up before the French goal. Bosquier cleared the ball, but it rolled over the line and Germany received a corner kick. Nobody scores anymore on corner kicks, and the French defense loomed high and powerful.

Schroeder's kick went up, came down. As it did, Otto Schoen, the German winger, crashed in like an American tackle blocking a punt. Short, square, Otto was the retriever, the uninspired but ever dependable man of the German team. He threw his compact frame into that wall of French defenders, squeezed through, and headed the ball at the goal.

A French back headed it away. A German headed it back in. A Frenchman leaped up, a German hit it with his forehead. Ping . . . ping . . . ping . . . ping . . . the ball never touched the ground.

Then Borkowski, the halfback, tall and powerful, leaped high in the air above everyone and caught it squarely on his blond, flat head. But the shot struck the crossbar, bounced back, bobbled dangerously along the ground before the goal. Three men were on it, but Sepp Obermeyer, following it up like a cat, was first. With one quick blow of his foot he hammered it home. The score was tied.

Pandemonium shook the German stands, a kind of collective madness. Thousands of red-black-and-gold flags gyrated in the sunshine. Thousands of Bavarian hunting horns echoed in the air. Thousands of voices roared out his name.

"Sepp . . . Sepp . . . Sepp. . . ."

Yes, and Otto, too, who started it, the man you never noticed on the field, the player you always took for granted, Otto, steady, unspectacular, always taking the weight off his teammates by his tackles and pass interceptions. Sepp had scored the goal, but it had been invented by Otto.

Sepp. Otto. The Germans in the stands cheered them, jumped up and down in jubilation, and their teammates embraced the two men.

The French stood silent. Less than a minute left in the final half. Now for the first time France felt the pressure. Big Garnier leaned over in exhaustion, utterly spent, shaking his head in agonized disappointment. Even young Varin felt like a coasting car, moving without the motor running. He was still dangerous, but worn down by his efforts all afternoon.

Here the soundness of the baron's tactics told. Now Germany, elated at having tied the score, began to control play with an insolent competence. The halfbacks, the bombers, sure-footed and disciplined, rolled into action, their passes accurate, their position play perfect, despite the chewed-up turf. Now the Germans were the ones who seemed to have eyes in the back of their heads, often sending the ball to a spot they could not see, knowing a teammate would be there at the exact moment to receive it.

The unbearable tension increased. The stands were in an absolute frenzy. Each second was charged with electricity. The game was a fraction of a minute from the end.

It all began so innocuously, so innocently. Horst Heppner came downfield with the ball and threaded a pass to Schwartz. Speed told, for the entire French defense was caught on the hop. A tiny mistake, a failure of anticipation or lack of concentration due to overfatigue, a defender two feet behind instead of two feet ahead, and Germany was off.

Schwartz made a short, crisp pass to Heppner and received the ball back. Then, with the ball at his feet, he raced in a wide arc around two weary defenders. His speed was dazzling. Now he was in open territory and within twenty-five yards of the French net.

He sighted the goal and let go with his left foot. The ball was moving away from Bosquier, who made a desperate stab, rolling over and over on the ground as it shot past him.

An instant later the whistle blew. The game was over. Germany had won.

Chapter 9

Down on the field one man stood out for everyone to see.

Big Jules Garnier, the French captain, never shaved before an important match. Now his face was black with beard. Sweat poured from his forehead. His red jersey was filthy and torn. Panting, exhausted, he rushed up to Rudy Stampfli, still immaculate in his blue shorts, pointing at Heppner and arguing with what breath he had left.

The French stands, silent, horror-struck after that unexpected goal, understood immediately. Suddenly everyone took up the refrain. *"Faute! Faute! FAUTE!"*

Obviously Garnier was claiming offside on the last play. The Frenchman towered over the stocky little Swiss. Two, three, four French players, all equally positive and vehement, surrounded the referee as he stood with the ball under one arm.

There he remained, listening impassively, holding his ground, feet apart. Finally he moved away, shaking his head firmly. Then someone caught his free arm and spun him around. He was face to face with Bosquier, the goalkeeper, a hot-headed Marseillais.

"*Nein . . . nein . . . nein. . . .*" Even from the press box you could see Rudy Stampfli's expression and the set of his jaw.

"*NEIN!*" There it was. The goal was good. No, there was no German offside on the play. The score stands. The game is over, done, lost, and won.

By this time French troops had swarmed all over the field and were encircling the German players to protect them from an ugly, menacing crowd that had poured down from the stands.

The enraged French fans, milling around on the turf shouted at the Germans and the referee. Good sense, fair play were not at the moment in them. To a man they honestly believed that France had been cheated.

Look, they cried to one another, what can you expect? Rudy is from Zurich. I don't trust the German-

Swiss. Had he been from Geneva, from the Suisse Romande, things would have been different. You know, everyone claims he was a friend of the baron's family, that he knew the von Kleinschrodts before the war. Besides he often played against him. It's unfair. The referee should have been Dutch or English or Spanish or Portuguese or even a Macaroni.

Why anyone could see that German halfback was plainly offside on that pass. Otherwise Jules would have caught him and cut him down. France was robbed by that second goal.

Still Stampfli shook his head, pushing away the French players. Still the angry fans howled at the Germans and hurled imprecations at the referee. Soldiers formed a tight ring around Stampfli and the victorious team and forced a passage through the mob. So into a tunnel under the stands they went, past the back of the stadium where in improvised cubbyholes sportswriters were dictating copy to Berlin, Madrid, or Rome.

"*Ne coupez pas, mademoiselle, ne coupez pas!*" screamed an agonized voice.

"*Und dann . . . Varin . . . nein, nein. Varin . . . V-A-R-I-N.*"

"Final score: Germany two, France one. Yes, that's the final. Germany scored in the last second of the game."

The hot, sweaty, exhausted players and the Swiss

referee, as emotionally drained as any of them, rushed by these reporters hard at work and were hustled over to a German bus that was standing and waiting, its engine running, a driver at the wheel.

Beside the bus was a row of police cars and army jeeps. Helmeted soldiers sat in each jeep, cradling tommy guns on their knees. The players' clothes, bags, and personal belongings had already been loaded, and one by one with Stampfli they filed aboard and sank into a seat. Soon the bus filled up. Behind it was a smaller vehicle a Volkswagon minibus. Into it piled five players who could not get into the larger bus: the baron, Otto Schoen, Sepp Obermeyer, Helmut Herberger, and young Schroeder, the centre forward.

The troops formed a cordon around the two buses, letting nobody near. In three minutes they were off. All traffic was held up to let them get away. The buses swung out with their armed escort ahead and behind, crossed the Seine, and went down a long, straight avenue lined with poplar trees. For twenty minutes they rolled along at a good speed, the jeeps leading the way with honking horns, the police cars following. About fifteen miles from the city and well out into the countryside, they turned into a long driveway leading to a large hotel. Everybody climbed out. Clothes and bags were unloaded, and they all filed into the hotel where the manager passed out keys to rooms with baths on the upper floors.

174

An hour later they piled back into the buses and the caravan set out again. They had been told to avoid the main roads and take the coastal highway to the frontier. So they rode for an hour through the radiant spring countryside, and when they reached the sea the jeeps and police car honked several times, pulled over, turned around, and left.

Now the two buses went on alone, headed for Munich and its streets packed with thousands upon thousands of celebrating football fans.

Chapter 10

The point of playing a game is to win. To fight hard, to play fairly, but to win. Otherwise, what on earth is the use? Defeat kills a great athlete. Defeat is numbing. It silences a dressing room after a game, renders everyone speechless. Defeat is humbling, obscene.

But victory is sweet. When you also play well in a game it is sweeter. Every man in that minibus from young Helmut Herberger to the veteran Otto Schoen had played a part in the triumph. Each one was elated. Each one had given his best. Had they not beaten a better team, stopped young Varin and held him to a single goal?

Inter of Milan couldn't do that! Nor Real of Madrid, either!

How quickly, when one wins, the aches and pains, the bone weariness, the bruises, and the hurts are forgotten. They sat there, not singing and cheering as their teammates were doing ahead in the larger bus, which was now almost lost on the horizon, but suffused in happiness. Each man savored the moments, remembering that pass, that stop, that last final team rush downfield. Yes, they were a team, by God; they had played as a team, won as a team. As they had done all year in Germany against the rest of the league, as they had done against Torpedo Dynamo of Moscow and Chelsea Bridge of London. The world was warm. The world always is when you want badly to win and finally do.

They rode in silence: dependable Otto, Sepp Obermeyer, with a bruise across his forehead, Helmut Herberger, Schroeder, the centre forward, his blond hair standing straight up after the shower he had taken in the hotel, and the baron, exhausted, slumped in his seat. They were happy, relaxed, anxious only to get out of France and reach home. The straight road led along the coast as far as they could see, winding up and along the dunes and cliffs and headlands in the distance. The larger bus by this time was so far ahead it had vanished. They were alone.

Soon they passed concrete blockhouses that once, long ago, had been part of Rommel's famous Atlantic wall. Some were now tilted upward at weird angles, their guns pointing harmlessly at the sky. Others were mounds of rubble. Still others were untouched, remaining exactly as they were when their garrisons filed out with hands behind heads in surrender twenty years before.

The players watched them slip past uneasily. This was a defeat they preferred to ignore.

They went up a hill. The sea was smooth and calm in the evening light of June. Then the minibus rolled into a village of one street, the children parting in the road to watch it go by. All at once the bus slowed, groaned, stopped dead.

The driver shook his head in exasperation. "Ah, that damned magneto again."

He opened the door, got down, and raised the hood in the rear. Immediately a crowd of youngsters gathered to watch. Behind the driver the players rose, stretched, and filed slowly into the street. The last man out was the baron. You could tell how stiff and sore he was by the careful way he left the bus, how he held the door handle as he descended.

Ernst, the driver, was now underneath the vehicle, and Sepp, who knew engines, was leaning down and talking to him. Just ahead, beside a low seawall, was a monument. The baron walked over and looked at it.

Nothing ornate, nothing overdone, the monument was neither elaborate nor expensive. It consisted of a slab of roughly hewn granite topped by a granite arm and fist rising into space. High above the water, it must have been visible far out at sea. Silhouetted against the sky, the stone fist held a sword broken just above the hilt.

On the slab was a metal plaque. Twenty years of moisture-laden fogs had weathered it so badly that it was barely legible. The baron bent down. With difficulty he made out names of those who had been his enemies, his friends.

MORT POUR LA FRANCE

———

June 5, 1944

———

Georges Varin, *Instituteur*
Le Père Clement, *Prêtre*
Charles Lavigne, *Gérant*
Louis Marquet, *Agriculteur*
Marcel Deschamps, *Pécheur*
René Le Gallec, *quinze ans, Étudiant*

My God, thought the baron, this is Nogent-Plage! We're on the Grande Rue and it is the fifth of June!

179

Chapter 11

Young Schroeder and Herberger joined him before the monument, leaning over to read the lettering on the plaque. What could it possibly mean to these boys? the baron wondered. They were but a few years old when it all happened, twenty years ago to the day.

The children of the village, openly curious, surrounded the strangers from the stranded bus. Once again the baron reflected, as he had so often in the past, on how appealing were the French youngsters. The boys wore shorts and striped jerseys, the girls checked dresses and wide-brimmed straw hats.

Like everyone else in the home town of Jean-Paul

Varin, these children had spent the afternoon watching the game. Therefore, the face of Otto Schoen, the crewcut of Sepp Obermeyer, above all the lined, handsome features of the baron were familiar to them.

One boy, bolder than the others, edged toward the big man and with up-turned face asked, "Are you Monsieur the Baron von Kleinschrodt?"

For a minute the man almost shook his head. Then looking down at the child, he realized this boy could have been the son of René Le Gallec, had René Le Gallec lived and played for France. The denial died away in his throat. At least he owed the truth to those six whose names were on the simple monument. So he nodded.

Elated, the boy shrieked, jumping up and down, "Laurent! Kiki! Jules! *Viens vite! Le Baron est à* Nogent-Plage."

They came from nowhere, they scrambled up the cliff, they swarmed about him, thrusting bits of paper and grubby pencils at him. Others rushed from their houses to join the group. He stood there signing his name, hearing as he did that familiar half slap, half crunch of the waves on the pebbly beach below. It took him back to that distant June afternoon, that day which began in such calm and quiet and ended in such disaster for everyone concerned. Suddenly he felt a jab in his sore ribs. It was the more painful side,

181

where he had fallen and perhaps injured himself. It hurt. He looked up angrily.

Before his face were the eyes of a madman. It was more than mere madness; there was ferocity in those eyes, a kind of animal savagery. The man had quite obviously not shaved for a week. His hair was long and matted. In his hands was a hunting rifle. It felt most uncomfortable against the baron's ribs.

The children immediately explained. "Ah, it's only Pierre. Crazy Pierre, Monsieur the Baron, don't take any notice of him."

"It's only Pierre Marquet. Don't worry. . . ."

"He was in a prison camp five years. He's touched in the head. . . ."

So the demented son of old Louis Marquet stood there, holding a deadly weapon, and incredibly, as if the madman simply did not exist, the boys kept after the baron for his autograph. The baron was a famous football player, the same as Jean-Paul. They had heard their elders talk about him many times in connection with the killing of six hostages from the village during the war. But to the children, the hostages were merely names on a monument, whereas the baron was a living legend, someone everybody had watched that afternoon on TV, the incredible German goalkeeper.

Suddenly Crazy Pierre was joined by a biggish man, also with an insane look in his eyes. He, too, had a weapon, a tommy gun cradled in his arm.

The boys spoke up. "It's the Racleur. The fiddler. He was at Dachau five years. He's mad, too."

Vaguely the baron remembered a village youth who had assaulted a German officer when he was picked up in a labor sweep at Verville. That was all. How strange he should remember.

A big, wild-faced woman joined the growing circle. Her straggly hair blew about in the wind. The baron had recognized her coming down the street. She carried a small pistol which once belonged to some German officer.

Her voice was grating, menacing. "So, you have returned! You have dared to come back!" She next addressed herself to what was now a sizable crowd of villagers, young and old, crying out that the *Herr Oberst* had pretended to be a friend and then butchered her only son, René. Her rapid French was much too fast for any of the Germans but the baron to follow. She was taking over and the crowd was with her, stirring uneasily at her words.

"Monsieur Le Boucher," she suddenly screamed. She motioned the baron ahead with her pistol. Crazy Pierre and the Racleur aped her gesture with their weapons. He moved along with his teammates and the minibus driver beside him.

On both sides of the street the wooden shutters of second-story windows flew open with that whanging sound he recalled so well. Women leaned out to watch. "*Herr Oberst,*" they said, pointing at him.

"*Herr Oberst.*" They did not say it in a polite, pleasant fashion as they used to long ago. Now they mouthed the old familiar name in a brutal, savage way. The strange procession moved up the Grande Rue, followed by every child in town.

That house there was the home of the widow Dupont. She must be dead by now. She had a small white fox terrier, which stood outside yapping at everyone who passed. He never yapped at me; he knew I liked dogs. That's where the Bleu Marin used to be. I see they call it the Café des Mariniers now. The awning is yellow and the chairs outside are different. I always liked those old iron ones.

Schroeder, Herberger, Obermeyer, Schoen, and the driver looked at him. What's up? Where are they taking us? He had no idea, save that it was ridiculous. They must all be mad.

They paused before an unoccupied stone house. It was the Bloch villa.

Someone kicked roughly at the front door. It crashed open. They were all pushed inside by the insane French with their guns. The room on the right, he could dimly see, had been his headquarters. They were shoved down a flight of steps into the cellar, dark and dank, a dirty floor underfoot. This, he recalled, had been where those six hostages had huddled while he sat upstairs in the office so tormented and alone.

184

The five other Germans surrounded him, asking questions. What does it all mean? Who are these crazy people with guns? Did the end of the game upset them this much? Do they take football that seriously? What's the matter with them? The baron's teammates knew, of course, that he was the so-called Butcher of Nogent-Plage. What they did not know was that this was Nogent-Plage. So what's going on, Herr Hans?

Footsteps echoed overhead. Then Madame Le Gallec's voice could be heard giving orders. She was obviously in command. But what was happening? The minutes seemed eternal. Just so, thought the baron, they must have seemed to those five Frenchmen and a boy in this same cellar twenty years before.

Chapter 12

The little red Renault rolled along the back roads, following almost exactly the same course the two German buses had taken half an hour before. The packed crowd around the French dressing room had given Jean-Paul a tremendous ovation when he appeared, and the police had to wedge a path to his parked car. Now, out in the country, with his mother beside him, the bitterness of defeat still hung over his heart.

She knew how desperately he had wanted victory in that match and how badly he felt. So she said little at first. Then, as they spun along toward Nogent-Plage, as they drew farther and farther from the stadium, from the crowd and the noise and the scarred turf, above all from the black depression which had pervaded the dressing room, he began to answer briefly.

"Yes, to play well is satisfying. I did my best. But I was playing today for France. I was part of a team."

"The whole team played well. You deserved to win."

"Both teams played well; both deserved to win." There was a hardness, a bleakness about his voice. Unfortunately he was right. Both teams deserved to win and fate had not smiled upon France.

She tried to change the subject. "You know the thing that amazed me about him?" No need to explain to whom she referred. "He seems so little changed. Prison and all the years since the war haven't greatly altered him. How did he look close up?"

"Like Gibraltar. Like the world's best goalie. Put him on our side, and we would have won by six to ten points. Not that Georges Bosquier isn't a good goalkeeper; he is, the best in France. But the baron today . . . well, I've never seen anything like it and nobody else has either."

She was silent for several miles. He was right; nobody had ever seen such a goalie in action before.

"You know, Jean-Paul, I've always felt all my life that there was something different about the Germans, even about the *Herr Oberst*, even before that day. . . . He . . . you see . . . they've been our enemies. . . ."

The young man shrugged his shoulders. "Oh, *Maman*, they are no different from ourselves. They want to win; they would always give anything to beat us. We too wanted to win; we gave everything to beat them and failed. As a boy I felt we would never do the things the Germans did to us during the war. Then came our colonial wars, in Vietnam and in Algeria. Oh, especially in Algeria. Tortures. Massacres. Cruelty. Dropping bombs on innocent villages. You see the point is that everyone loses control in a war. Sometimes in sport, too."

They were coming to the sea now, and it was calm in the June evening. Madame Varin started to protest. Surely this was going a bit far. She pointed out that the Algerian war was not the same as a World War.

"You must realize, Jean-Paul, Algeria was a *département* of France. It had been so ever since 1830 . . . a long time, my boy."

He was tired, ravaged by defeat when victory had been so close he could taste it. Although he loved his mother and tried to be patient, he burst out, "Yes, of course I know. Did I not hear this repeated a hundred times in school, in books, in the newspapers! I know it all. I can say it by heart, like every French schoolboy. I learned about the army that landed at Sidi-Ferraud on June 14, 1830. About the Insurrection of 1871 and the creation of the new *département* of Algeria. I know it all. But what is the fact? The fact is that we invaded North Africa and colonized it. We subjugated the people. . . ."

"But Jean-Paul, surely Algeria is different. It had been French for over a hundred years. Even the Moslems were French citizens."

"Yes, they were French citizens, and they were allowed to serve in our armed forces and die for France. What other rights did they have? Algeria had been settled by French *colons* for a hundred years. . . ."

"My boy, you forget the Maréchal Lyautey. And how the Moslems prayed for him in their mosques during the war with the Riff and how they sobbed openly in the streets at his death. Ah, you are far too young to remember these things."

"*Maman, chère Maman,* I know about the *maréchal.* He built Morocco into a fruitful consumer for French products."

How stubborn he was, she thought, how exactly like his father with these strange ideas of Marxism and equality. "Jean-Paul, you forget that we poured money, French money, into North Africa, and lives too, thousands of them, some of our noblest and best, men who had the interests of the North Africans at heart."

"Spare me, *Maman,*" he said, fatigue in his voice.

"True, we poured money into North Africa, but we took millions more from it. We. . . ."

His mother interrupted. "Look! What's that? Ahead, off to the right. It looks like a glow on the horizon. A fire, perhaps. Could it be in Nogent-Plage?"

He looked ahead. There was a slight glow in the distance over the cliffs. "Well, it could be. But most likely it is Varengeville. They're forever having fires there. We'll be able to tell when we get around the next headland."

He increased the little car's speed. They zipped along the empty coastal road toward the glow in the distance. Soon it became larger. Yes, it could be Nogent-Plage.

Chapter 13

The whole town was in the Grande Rue as he pulled up with his mother in the red Renault. They almost dragged him from behind the wheel, raised him to their shoulders, carried him up the street past the smoldering ruin of the Volkswagon minibus, twisted and charred.

"Var . . . IN! Var . . . IN! Var . . . IN!"

He's ours. Ours, you understand, ours from Nogent-Plage. Win or lose, the greatest centre forward in all Europe, the best France has ever produced. Born right here in this village, too.

"Var . . . IN! Var . . . IN! Var . . . IN!"

At first the noise and excitement and the faces of

the crowd confused Jean-Paul. What was it? What was happening? There was a smell of smoke in the air. In agitated tones a half-dozen voices shouted the explanation.

"They burned the bus, Jean-Paul. The bus that was carrying the Fritz back to Germany. The Germans cheated this afternoon at Rouen. They cheated. . . ."

"Crazy Pierre started it. . . ."

"He has the Germans locked up in the cellar of the Bloch villa, Jean-Paul. . . ."

Now he began to understand. Something evil was happening. The evil could be seen in those faces. Immediately he forced his way down from their shoulders as they crowded about, yelling and cheering, echoing the same cry that had resounded over the Stade Rouennais that afternoon.

"Var . . . IN! Var . . . IN! Var . . . IN!"

"But attention! Listen to me! Those German players. . . ."

"Oh they're under lock and key in that cellar. And their baron, too. Ah, let me tell you the Feldwebel Hans is locked up in the cellar for a change. *Et comment!* We have him. Let him fry with the others."

"Jean-Paul, Madame Le Gallec and Pierre are going to burn the place to the ground. . . ."

"But you can't do that!"

"We will. We are doing it already. We are burning that foul building where such harm was done in Nogent-Plage. And the baron shot your father, didn't he? Didn't he? He murdered six people from this town. Then this afternoon the Germans cheated; that's why they won. France was the better team. Everyone knew it, everyone could see it. . . ."

Jean-Paul shoved, pushed, worked his way out of the embraces, the back slapping, toward the Bloch villa. Crazy Pierre was carrying hay on a pitchfork, evidently to supplement the fire that he and Madame Le Gallec had started, that now was beginning to blaze up in earnest. The boy knew the madman was capable of anything.

He fought through the crowd and stood facing them on the steps of the villa. It was easy to see the fever in their eyes. This was a mob, led in whole or in part by Crazy Pierre, and the mob was momentarily insane. He raised his hand and shouted at the top of his lungs, "Listen to me! Listen to me!"

Behind him he heard the crackle of old paint. He could smell the ancient wainscoting burning.

"Friends, neighbors, we must stop this insanity. We cannot. . . ."

"Jean-Paul, he killed your father," a woman screamed. "He murdered six of us."

"He shot my boy, René," Madame Le Gallec cried. "He shot your father, too."

For a second Jean-Paul realized this sickness was the same malady which had swept the French stands in Rouen that afternoon. "Look, my friends. Today I was hurt. I was sore, bruised, inside and out. . . ." Hurry, hurry, he thought to himself, in a few minutes it will be too late. "I also felt bitter towards those Germans. But we cannot take human lives. What would my father say, I ask you? He was a humanist; he would have told us we cannot continue to cherish grudges. If we keep feeding on these hatreds handed down to us by our ancestors, our grandfathers and great grandfathers, where are we? Friends, what good are wars? Who ever won a war? Who ever profited from them in the end?"

Slowly the madness that hung over the mob seemed to diminish and even the anger in the faces lessened. He could feel the decent people on the far edges of the crowd asserting themselves. Why, Jean-Paul is right. We cannot murder these men. We must not let them die in the cellar.

"Friends! Marcel! Pierre! Yves, you knew my father. You, Madame Bonnet, you also knew him. Reflect! There were six French in that cellar twenty years ago. Now, in the same cellar, we have six Germans. Shall we do to them what they did to us? If so, how are we different from those who murdered my father? If we kill them, we are guilty of the same crime. Somehow, somewhere, we must break this evil chain and look on each other as human beings."

He seized the moment of their hesitation, turned abruptly, rushed at the door. Crazy Pierre barred the way. Jean-Paul gave him a body block, tore the rifle from his grasp, and threw it to the street. He rushed into the hallway. One thrust of his powerful right leg knocked a cellar door panel loose. There was sufficient space for the Germans to squeeze through.

"Quick! Quick, for God's sake, or the building will fall in on us all!"

"Here, Sepp, give me your hand."

Then he pulled Otto through and young Herberger, frightened and babbling something to him. Someone was beside him now, attacking the door with an axe. It cracked, splintered, burst apart. Another panting German stepped out and another. Last of all came the baron.

Through the smoke in the light of the blaze, the German recognized Varin and threw his arms around him.

"Jean-Paul, believe me! I did not give the order to fire. I did not kill your father."

He held the younger man tight. Varin in turn clasped him. He nodded. *"Oui, je sais, je sais,"* he said. I know. I know.

Once outside in the crisp sea air the Germans staggered about, limp and dazed, some trembling. But the dementia of the moment seemed to have passed. That evil atmosphere seemed to have vanished. Villagers were helping the German athletes and the minibus driver, supporting them, leading them away from the fire. A woman brought them water from a bucket.

Now, except for Crazy Pierre and the widow Le Gallec, who was still screaming about the Butcher of Nogent-Plage, everybody was quiet, chastened, frightened as they perceived how narrowly a tragedy had been averted. Inside the Bloch villa the flames hissed and roared, but hoses were now playing into the windows. The danger was past.

Jean-Paul and the baron had appeared on the steps with their arms around each other's shoulders. Now they stood across the street from the burning building, still with their arms around each other's shoulders. It was difficult to tell who was supporting whom.

Then quick, explicit, unmistakable came the sound of the shot. The baron's hand went up, clutching his temple. He spun around and tumbled to the pavement at Varin's feet.

"Ah . . ." a collective groan came from them all as Crazy Pierre raced down the Grande Rue, waving his rifle in the air.

There lay the man. Jean-Paul looked at the red puncture on his forehead from which the blood was pouring. He slipped down beside him weeping, beside the dead body of his enemy, his friend.

John R. Tunis was born in Cambridge, Massachusetts, and graduated from Harvard. After the end of World War I, during which he served in France, he wrote sports for the *New York Evening Post*, covering athletic events here and abroad. He has written over 2,000 articles—on sports, education, and other subjects—which have appeared in leading American magazines.

Over the years he has crossed the Atlantic fifty times, lived in France, and speaks French and Spanish. He is also the author of twenty novels for young people. His book, *American Girl*, was made into a movie by RKO in 1951. Mr. Tunis lives in eastern Connecticut.